THE INTERVIEW

BEHIND THE DIGITAL CURTAIN

SOUMYA MONDAL

To fellow cyberdefenders, your tireless efforts against unseen threats safeguard this intricate digital world.

Contents

Foreword   vii

Preface   ix

Acknowledgements   xi

Prologue   xiii

1. Behind The Firewall: A Cyber Warrior's Fire   1

2. Navigating The Digital Battlefield: Frameworks And Tactics In The Cybersecurity Arena   8

3. Navigating The Digital Archipelago: Platforms, Frameworks, And The Elusive Fortress   21

4. Beyond The Breach: Minimizing The Blast Radius   42

5. Guardians At The Gates: Building Ethical AI Defenses For The Digital Fortress   60

6. Beyond AI: The Unsung Hero - Secure Software Coding Security   81

7. Beyond Uptime: Cultivating Organizational Resilience And Digital Operations   97

8. Building The Resilient Fortress: Bricks Of Policy, Mortar Of Framework, And The Spirit Of Practice   117

9. Building Bridges, Not Backdoors: Fostering Collaboration And Trust In The Digital Ecosystem   133

10. Shifting Tides: A Shared Journey Of Growth Begins   142

Beyond the Scoreboard: Redefining Talent in the Age of AI   149

FOREWORD

Welcome you, intrepid traveler, to the ever-evolving, ever-challenging realm of cybersecurity. Here, where data reigns supreme and vulnerabilities lurk in every shadow, only the sharpest minds and most resilient spirits can truly thrive. However, no need to sweat, for within these pages there is a roadmap, a guideline in the form of "The Interview."

Think of this book not as a dry academic tome, but as a gripping conversation – a simulated job interview where you, the aspiring cybersecurity warrior, stand face-to-face with seasoned veterans. Each question delves into the intricate facets of this multifaceted domain, from the tried-and-true bastions of traditional security to the nebulous frontiers of cloud protection and the enigmatic world of AI-powered defense.

Through these simulated exchanges, you will grapple with the ever-shifting sands of risk and compliance, learn to wield the potent tool of threat modeling, and discover the double-edged sword that is Chat GPT security. Each answer, a brushstroke against the canvas of your knowledge, paints a clearer picture of your preparedness, your mettle, your aptitude for navigating the labyrinthine pathways of this critical field.

But be warned, dear reader. "The Interview" is not merely a test of technical ability. It is a crucible that tempers your critical thinking, hones your communication skills, and ignites your passion for this vital pursuit. It forces you to confront not just the "what" and "how" of cybersecurity, but the "why." Why does it matter? Why dedicate your intellect and energy to this endless struggle?

The answer, you will soon discover, lies not in lines of code or impenetrable firewalls, but in the very fabric of our connected world. It is about protecting the privacy of individuals, the integrity of information, the very heartbeat of the digital age. It is about standing guard against the shadows, ensuring that the promise of technology remains bright, unyielding, and forever out of reach of malicious intent.

So, take a deep breath, sharpen your intellect, and step into the virtual interview room. Let "The Interview" be your training ground, your proving ground, your launchpad into the exhilarating, ever-evolving world of cybersecurity. Remember, the future of the digital realm rests not just on the shoulders of seasoned veterans, but on the minds and hearts of those who dare to answer the call, who dare to enter the labyrinth – and emerge triumphant.

Onward, then, brave aspirant. The interview awaits.

Preface

The digital age has woven itself into the very fabric of our lives. Even the most ordinary moments, from our morning coffee to the cogs of international trade, are powered by the silent symphony of ones and zeros. Yet, amidst this digital harmony, a discordant note appears – the constant specter of cyber threats.

For most, the world of cybersecurity is a labyrinthine realm, shrouded in technical jargon and veiled by the mystique of digital frontiers. This book, however, serves as a torchbearer, illuminating the path for those seeking to navigate its complexities. Within its pages, you will not find yourself lost in a quagmire of intimidating code or overwhelmed by esoteric technical intricacies. Instead, you will embark on a journey guided by clear explanations, practical insights, and real-world scenarios.

Whether you are a seasoned security professional seeking to sharpen your skills, a curious novice yearning to understand the digital battlefield, or simply a concerned citizen safeguarding your online life, this book welcomes you with open arms. It caters to diverse needs, offering foundational knowledge for the uninitiated while simultaneously delving into advanced concepts for the experienced.

Here, you will delve into the minds of cyber adversaries, unraveling their motivations and dissecting their tactics. You will discover practical measures to fortify your digital defenses, from securing personal devices to safeguarding critical infrastructure. We will explore the forefront of cybersecurity, examining emerging technologies and anticipating future threats. And through compelling case studies and relatable examples, you will witness the practical application of theoretical knowledge, learning from both successes and failures in the real world.

This book delves beyond dry instructions, offering insights and practical applications. It is a call to action, an invitation to become an active participant in building a safer digital future. Cybersecurity is not merely the domain of tech giants and government agencies; it is a collective responsibility we all share. Let knowledge be our weapon, empowerment our shield, as we forge a brighter, safer digital future together.

So, join me as we embark on this vital journey. Turn the page, embrace the challenges, and prepare to become a vigilant citizen of the digital realm. By collaborating, we can transform the perilous landscape of cyber threats into a secure and interconnected digital worlds for all.

Onward, to a safer digital world!
Soumya Mondal

Acknowledgements

The journey to complete this book has been akin to piecing together a vibrant tapestry, each thread representing the invaluable contributions of those who made it possible. A heartfelt thank you to my invaluable mentors and colleagues, whose contributions have been instrumental in shaping my path. Their knowledge and insights have been a true inspiration. Your guidance, insightful critiques, and collaborative spirit shaped this book in countless ways. Your names may not appear on the cover, but your fingerprints are etched upon every page.

A special thank you to the security researchers and practitioners who tirelessly toil on the frontlines of this digital war. Your dedication to understanding and thwarting cyber threats inspires me every day. Thank you for inspiring me and countless others.

And finally, to the readers who pick up this book and embark on this journey with me, my sincerest gratitude. It is for you that I poured my heart and soul into these pages. I hope you find within them the knowledge, insights, and inspiration to navigate the ever-evolving landscape of cybersecurity. Your voices and informed choices empower us to create a safer digital world, together.

This book stands as a beacon, showing what we can achieve when we unite. Thank you.

Soumya Mondal

Prologue

The screen flickered, a constellation of emerald green characters dancing into existence against the inky blackness. Not code, not prose, but a language whispered in the shadows, the dialect of digital predators. In the sterile silence of the data center, the hum of cooling fans amplified the tension, a symphony of anticipation as I traced the digital footprints, each click a beat in the heart of a brewing cyber storm.

It started like a wisp of smoke, an anomaly detected deep within the network, a blip on the radar that sent shivers down the spines of seasoned security analysts. A rogue access point, a whisper of unauthorized traffic, then silence. The calm before the storm, we called it, a collective breath held as we waited for the next move, the inevitable escalation.

Days bled into nights, fueled by stale coffee and adrenaline. Sleep became a luxury we dared not afford as we delved into the labyrinthine digital trails, each twist and turn revealing a deeper layer of the attacker's insidious web. Malware woven with dark genius, camouflaged within the very fabric of our systems, poised to unleash chaos at the blink of a digital eye.

This was not just another breach, not a petty theft of data or a juvenile hack. This was a calculated strike, a surgical incision aimed at the very heart of our infrastructure, a message etched in cybernetic scars. The stakes had never been higher, the potential fallout a chilling cascade of frozen accounts, crippled systems, and lives hanging in the digital balance.

This prologue, dear reader, is not just the opening chapter of a book. It is a baptism by fire, an invitation to step into the shoes of those who stand guard at the digital gates, the sentinels in the ever-evolving cyberwars. Within these pages, you will witness the invisible battles fought in the silent realm of ones and zeros, the strategies unfurled and countered, the victories hard-won and the losses keenly felt. You will hear the whispers of the attackers, the cold logic of their motives, and the unwavering resolve of those who stand between them and the vulnerable heart of our digital lives.

So, turn the page, if you dare. Brace yourself for a plunge into the murky depths of the cyber warfront, where shadows dance and lines blur between heroes and villains. This is more than just a story; it is a call to arms, a reminder that in the digital age, vigilance is our only shield, and knowledge our most potent weapon. Welcome to the fight.

I

Behind the Firewall: A Cyber Warrior's Fire

Sunlight streamed through the high windows, painting warm squares on the polished mahogany table. Across it, Emili, fresh-faced and eager, leaned forward, her gaze intent on the man opposite her. His name was Soham, and his resume lay before her, a testament to a career steeped in the arcane world of cybersecurity.

"So, Mr. Soham," Emili began in her usual professional tone, "your experience in threat analysis is undeniable. But what truly drives your dedication to this unseen battlefield? What fuels your fire when you are chasing shadows in the digital abyss?"

Soham held his eye contact, a flicker of defiance challenging the stager's stoicism. "It's the unnoticeable stakes, Ms. Emili," he countered. "Protecting lives, not just data. Defending the invisible threads that bind our modern world, from the flicker of a hospital monitor to the drone guiding a surgeon's hand across continents."

He gestured towards the air, as if conjuring the digital landscape. "Each line of software code, each network point, holds the eventuality for chaos. It's a constant dance, anticipating the moves of unseen adversaries, weaving intricate defenses against their ever-evolving tactics."

His voice grew impassioned, his eyes catching the glint of the cityscape through the window.

"There is exhilaration, of course, in the intellectual hoodwink, the adrenaline rush of the chase. But it is the human cost that fuels my fight, Ms. Emili. The families shielded from financial ruin, the hospitals kept functioning, the secrets protected from falling into the wrong hands."

Emili's stoic facade softened, a hint of respect glinting in her eyes. "A worthy cause indeed, Mr. Soham," he conceded. "The unseen battleground needs custodians with your fervor, those who know the personal stories threaded into the digital edifice."

Emili resumed. "Your fidelity to protecting lives is truly inspiring. Can you share a specific case that solidified your commitment to this imperceivable battleground? A moment where the human impact of a cyberattack truly hit home for you?" This question allures Soham to share a personal story that showcases his emotional investment in cybersecurity and adds a layer of susceptibility to his character.

"Early in my career, I worked on a case where a hospital network was compromised. Hackers gained access to patient records, including diagnoses and medication information. While we managed to contain the breach, fear and uncertainty was on the faces of those patients. It was something I would never forget. That day, I realized the true weight of our responsibility in cybersecurity. We're not just defending data; we're safeguarding lives, livelihoods, and peace of mind."

"There was another incident, where we intercepted a cyberattack targeting a power grid. The attackers planned to cause widespread blackouts, potentially putting lives at risk during a harsh winter. Working through the night, my team and I managed to thwart their attempt. Seeing the news reports the next morning about the averted disaster - that's the kind of validation that keeps me going in this relentless fight."

"Thank you for articulating such personal stories, Mr. Soham", Emili responded in calm voice. "They truly explicate the abysmal cogency your work has on people's lives. Seeing your fidelity firsthand is incredibly motivating". "Still in both cases, you adduced coursing complicated ethical considerations. Were there moments where you had to make difficult choices between protecting individual privacy and potentially averting greater harm? How do you deal with those moral dilemmas in your work?"

Soham ceased for a moment and took a deep breath, a hint of amenability in his eyes, admitting the emotional weight of such choices.

"Absolutely, Ms. Emili. In a recent case, we intercepted a cyberattack targeting a financial institution. The attackers threatened to release sensitive customer data unless their demands were met. It was a brutal calculus: expose private information for potential financial ruin or remain silent and risk widespread panic and economic instability."

"We spent countless hours debating, consulting legal experts, and weighing the potential consequences. We opted for a targeted intervention, disrupting the attack before the data could be leaked. It was not a perfect solution, and we still grapple with the potential implications for individual privacy. But in that moment, the potential for widespread harm felt too great to ignore", he continued.

"So, Mr. Soham, what strategy did you use to deal with the obstacle?".

This question prompted Soham to adopt a more analytical tone, unfolding his established approach to ethical dilemmas. "In my experience, Ms. Emili, navigating such situations requires a clear framework. We prioritize minimizing harm, focusing on solutions that protect the most vulnerable and mitigate collateral damage. It's a constant balancing act, and transparency is crucial."

He also continued elaborating on specific tools and protocols they used. "We have internal ethical panels, consulting external experts, and guidelines for constantly modernizing our decision- making frameworks grounded on evolving pitfalls and legal precedents. Open communication with stakeholders and affected individuals is also paramount."

"I can sense that your role to counter such attack was certainly complex." Emili paused before continuing again. "Can you throw some light on the legal arguments that ultimately informed your chosen approach? How did you balance the potential violation of individual privacy with the threat of widespread economic instability?", Emili asked, her voice thoughtful.

"It was indeed a tightrope walk, Ms. Emili. We consulted with legal experts extensively, ensuring our actions adhered to data privacy regulations and emergency protocols. The potential for widespread financial ruin, potentially affecting millions, tipped the scales. We implemented a targeted intervention, isolating and neutralizing the attackers before they could access sensitive data. However, we did inform the affected individuals about the breach and offered credit monitoring services as a precautionary measure."

Emili acknowledged his explanation, "Well, Mr. Soham, while your solution in the financial institution case seems commendable, do you acknowledge the potential long-term implications of setting a precedent for intervention in the face of privacy concerns? Have you considered alternative solutions that might address similar threats without compromising individual rights?"

Soham responded, his gaze steady, "Absolutely, Ms. Emili. We understand the concerns surrounding intervention and acknowledge the need for constant vigilance in protecting individual privacy. We actively participate in industry discussions and research initiatives aimed at developing robust cyber defenses that minimize privacy intrusion. Ideally, we strive for solutions that prevent attacks altogether, eliminating the need for such difficult choices. Ultimately, it is a continuous effort to adapt and innovate, striking a balance between security and individual rights in this ever-evolving digital landscape."

Emili's curiosity piqued, "The targeted intervention you mentioned in the financial institution case sounds intriguing. Can you walk me through the technical framework you utilized? How did you isolate the attackers without compromising sensitive data?"

Soham, relishing the technical exchange, replied, "We deployed a layered defense, Ms. Emili. Imagine placing a decoy network – a honeypot filled with tempting digital bait – to lure the attackers away from the real systems. While they were busy feasting on this simulated environment, we employed zero-day exploit mitigation techniques. Think of it like digital bodyguards trained to recognize and disarm never-before-seen weapons. These techniques essentially confined the attackers' malicious software within the honeypot, a sterile sandbox isolated from the core systems, effectively rendering them harmless."

Emili, impressed by the analogy, leaned in further. "That is ingenious! How do you stay ahead of these constantly evolving threats and develop such innovative countermeasures?"

Soham chuckled. "It is a thrilling chase. We are plugged into global threat intelligence communities, constantly analyzing attack patterns, and identifying emerging vulnerabilities. Our research team is like a digital SWAT unit, pushing the boundaries of defensive technologies. We experiment with advanced sandboxing techniques, train machine learning algorithms to sniff out anomalies, and even collaborate with ethical hackers – white hats, we call them – to probe our own defenses and identify potential weaknesses before the bad guys do." Emili nodded, her respect for Soham's expertise growing.

"But surely these interventions raise concerns about privacy. How do you ensure transparency and accountability in your operations?" Soham acknowledged the delicate balance.

"Transparency is our watchword." Soham firmly responded.

"We have a dedicated internal oversight committee that meticulously reviews every intervention, ensuring adherence to strict legal and ethical frameworks. Every action is meticulously logged. Logs reveal typical patterns of behavior on your systems. Deviations from preconfigured baseline often signal something unusual and potentially malicious. When an attack occurs, logs act like breadcrumbs, allowing security teams to identify the attack's origin, track its progression and understand attacker techniques. And if necessary, we disclose information to relevant authorities while upholding individual privacy rights. It's a constant tightrope walk, but one we take veritably seriously."

Sunlight streamed through the high windows, painting warm squares on the polished mahogany table. Across it, Emili, fresh-faced and eager, leaned forward, her gaze intent on the man opposite her. His name was Soham, and his resume lay before her, a testament to a career steeped in the arcane world of cybersecurity.

II

Navigating the Digital Battlefield: Frameworks and Tactics in the Cybersecurity Arena

The interview had transformed into a captivating duel of wits, a glimpse into the intricate world of cybersecurity and the dedicated guardians who stand watch on the digital frontier.

Emili, eager to delve deeper, leaned forward. "The ongoing transformation of the threat landscape presents unique challenges, Mr. Soham. Could you elaborate on some of the specific adversaries you encounter and the types of attacks you prepare for?"

Soham, invigorated by her inquisitiveness, grinned. "We face a motley crew, Ms. Emili. From opportunistic script kiddies deploying rudimentary malware to state-sponsored advanced persistent threats wielding custom-crafted zero-day exploits, the spectrum is diverse. We constantly grapple with social engineering scams designed to phish for credentials, distributed denial-of-service attacks aimed at crippling critical infrastructure, and even the looming threat of supply chain attacks infiltrating systems through seemingly innocuous software updates."

Emili, her brow furrowed in concern, interjected. "Those sound incredibly sophisticated. How do you prepare for such diverse and dynamic threats?"

"It's an ongoing arms race, Ms. Emili," Soham admitted. "We leverage ethical hacking to uncover system weaknesses, simulating diverse real-world attack scenarios. We employ sophisticated intrusion detection systems constantly sifting through network traffic for anomalies, and we train our analysts to recognize the subtle fingerprints of various attack vectors."

Emili, intrigued by the technical jargon, inquired further. "Penetration testing? Intrusion detection systems? It sounds like you're building a digital fortress."

Soham chuckled. "Indeed. However, true strength requires addressing vulnerabilities, not just building defenses. That is why we also prioritize continuous education and awareness training for our clients and the public at large. The best defense is often a vigilant populace equipped with the knowledge to recognize and thwart these digital threats. A successful democracy depends on its most informed and engaged citizens."

Emili, her eyes gleaming with intellectual curiosity; "Mr. Soham, your mention of various attack vectors piqued my interest. So, what kind of cyber-attack do you encounter most frequently?"

Soham, appreciating her focus, responded, "There are varieties of tactics and techniques that are used for breaching cyber defense. We see a lot of adversaries leveraging MITRE ATT&CK's Initial Access and Persistence categories. Spear phishing campaigns exploiting Credential Access remain a constant threat, often leading to Persistence mechanisms like web shells or scheduled tasks. We also encounter lateral movement techniques like Remote Desktop Protocol abuse and Windows Management Instrumentation exploitation."

Emili, fascinated by such an explanation, "That's insightful. However, I was wondering what MITRE ATT&CK is?"

Soham smiled. "Imagine the bad guys in a heist movie. They do not just smash through the front door. They scout, find weaknesses, may hack into the security system. MITRE ATT&CK is like a map of all those sneaky tactics and techniques attackers use, from the initial recon to stealing your data. It is not just for fancy Hollywood heists, though. Think of any software, any system – it is like a fortress, and ATT&CK shows you all the cracks and tunnels the bad guys might try to exploit. It is like a cheat sheet for defenders, helping them patch up those weaknesses and build stronger defenses. So, instead of waiting for the attack to happen, defenders can use ATT&CK to be proactive, anticipating attackers' moves and setting traps, of course, figuratively. It is like knowing the playbook of the other team, always one step ahead of their next move."

Emili immediately asked, "Then how do you guard against them?" Soham, eager to showcase comprehensiveness of defensive approach, explained,

"The NIST (National Institute of Standards and Technology) Risk Management Framework (RMF) is a cornerstone of our approach to identify, assess, and mitigate risks. For example, the Identify stage helps us map potential threats to specific ATT&CK techniques, allowing us to prioritize controls based on their effectiveness against those attackers' tactics, techniques, procedures (TTPs). NIST 800-53 controls like Multi-Factor Authentication and Controlled Use of Administrative Privileges directly address credential access attempts, while Security Awareness and Training bolsters our defenses against social engineering scams."

Emili, intrigued by the specific controls mentioned, pressed further. "So, you essentially map ATT&CK tactics to relevant NIST controls within the RMF framework?"

"Think of your digital world as a treasure chest," Soham responded. "Inside are your precious assets – data, systems, even your reputation. The chest has weak spots, though – vulnerabilities like unlocked latches or flimsy wood like software bugs or outdated systems. Lurking outside are threats – hungry pirates like malware or hackers – always scanning for an opening. That is where risk comes in. It is the chance those pirates snag your treasure, like the likelihood a flimsy latch gives way. Now, you have guards - security controls like firewall, intrusion monitoring systems that act like watchtowers. And some things, like your business blueprint and software codes are extra valuable, and therefore have high-asset value. So, you keep them in a hidden vault, like stronger encryption. It is a balancing act – understanding weaknesses, anticipating threats, and protecting what matters most, all to keep your digital treasure chest safe."

"That is fascinating. Is there a comparable situation where this has been applied successfully? Can you draw parallels?"

Soham, happy to delve deeper, recounted, "Recently, we faced an adversary attempting a lateral movement through the RDP. By referencing the ATT&CK matrix, we identified this as a technique within the Lateral Movement category. Leveraging the RMF, we analyzed our existing controls and implemented additional measures aligning with NIST 800-53's Security Measures for Information Systems and Organization control, specifically restricting RDP access and implementing network segmentation. This effectively thwarted the attacker's attempts and contained the potential damage."

Sunlight continued to stream through the window, casting long shadows that seemed to dance with the intricacies of their conversation. The interview had become a captivating exploration of the digital battlefield, revealing the tireless efforts of those who stand guard against unseen adversaries in the ever-evolving realm of cybersecurity.

Emili's gaze sharpened with focused curiosity. "Mr. Soham, your mention of specific NIST 800-53 controls like Multi-Factor Authentication and Controlled Use of Administrative Privileges for credential access was insightful. However, I am curious about how other controls contribute to your layered defense strategy."

Soham, relishing the deeper technical discussion, readily expounded, "We certainly do not rely solely on a few controls. Against the reconnaissance activities outlined in NIST 800-53, we prioritize Continuous Monitoring and Security Assessment Tools. These act as vigilant sentries, constantly scrutinizing network activity and system logs for suspicious behavior, snuffing out reconnaissance attempts before they escalate into full-blown attacks."

Emili, intrigued by the focus on specific attack stages, nodded. "That makes perfect sense. And for more advanced threats like lateral movement, what controls come into play?"

Soham grinned. "Ah, by dividing the network into smaller, isolated sections, segmentation effectively hinders attackers' ability to move laterally, aligning with the security principles outlined in the 'Information in Shared System Resources' control family. We meticulously carve up our networks into isolated zones, creating an intricate maze that restricts an attacker's ability to freely roam once they gain a foothold. Additionally, controls like Identification and Authentication and Physical and Logical Access Control ensure only authorized users and devices have access to specific zones, further hindering lateral movement."

Emili, impressed by the comprehensive approach, pressed further. "So, your control implementation seems to be tailored to the NIST 800-53 attack stages, from reconnaissance to exfiltration. Is that correct?"

Soham chuckled. "Precisely. It is like playing a multi-dimensional chess game against diverse adversaries. We analyze attack patterns, map them to relevant NIST categories, and then strategically deploy controls that address those specific stages and techniques. For instance, against command-and-control activities, we focus on controls like Security Event Management and System Monitoring, actively hunting for signs of attacker communication channels and isolating compromised systems before they become launchpads for further harm."

Emili's curiosity sharpened. "Mr. Soham, your explanation of the interplay between these frameworks is fascinating. But how do you translate this knowledge into tangible actions? How do organizations like yours utilize this knowledge to plan and execute effective red team vs blue team activities?"

Soham, relishing the shift towards practical application, grinned. "The synergy is remarkable. By mapping potential threats from MITRE ATT&CK to specific controls in NIST 800-53 through the RMF process, we create a simulated battlefield for Red Team exercises. We inject specific ATT&CK techniques, mimicking real-world adversaries, and observe how our Blue Team's deployed controls – firewalls, intrusion prevention systems, malware detection tools – fare against those simulated attacks."

Emili, her gaze intent, leaned forward. "That is ingenious! So, you essentially use these frameworks to tailor Red Team scenarios, testing the effectiveness of your chosen security controls in a controlled environment?"

Soham nodded enthusiastically. "Exactly! We can then analyze the Blue Team's response, identify any weaknesses in our control deployment or configuration, and refine our defenses accordingly. It is an iterative process, constantly honing our defenses based on real-world attack simulations."

Emili, impressed by the proactive approach, pressed further. "And what practical challenges does this present when it comes to rolling out security measures? Does this framework interplay guide your choices, say, between an intrusion prevention system and a network access control solution?"

Soham chuckled. "Absolutely! By mapping potential threats to specific controls, we can prioritize based on their effectiveness against those attack vectors. For instance, if we anticipate spear phishing attempts, we might prioritize multi-factor authentication and security awareness training. Similarly, if lateral movement is a concern, network segmentation and endpoint detection and response tools become crucial."

Emili, her eyes gleaming with understanding, nodded. "So, it is a data-driven approach, constantly evolving with the threat landscape. This integrated framework seems like a powerful tool for any organization looking to fortify its cybersecurity posture."

Soham smiled. "Indeed. It is not just about deploying the latest technology; it is about understanding the adversary, mapping threats to controls, and continuously testing and refining our defenses. These frameworks become the blueprints for building a resilient cybersecurity ecosystem."

Emili leaned forward; her eyes alight with curiosity. "Soham, your explication of how these frameworks work together paints a clear picture. But can you site any example how you have used them in Red Team exercises? Any specific case where they helped your blue team excel?"

Soham sneered, relishing the shift to factual examples. "Definitely! We recently conducted a Red Team exercise simulating a sophisticated Advanced Persistent Threat aka APT attack targeting an energy company. Using the MITRE ATT&CK framework, we mapped common APT tactics like spear phishing and lateral movement through RDP to specific NIST 800-53 controls like multi-factor authentication and network segmentation. This informed our Red Team's attack vector, mimicking real-world APT tactics."

Emili, captivated, hung on to his every word. "And did the Blue Team achieve their objectives?"

"The Red Team launched their attack with a well-designed phishing email, quickly establishing a foothold," Soham admitted. "However, implementing controls identified through the Risk Management Framework (RMF), we were able to contain the impact of the incident. Multi-factor authentication prevented unauthorized access beyond the compromised account, and network segmentation limited the attacker's lateral movement. Our Blue Team, armed with endpoint detection and response tools like Extended Detection and Response (EDR) and Security Information and Event Management (SIEM), quickly identified the anomaly and neutralized the threat before it could cause widespread disruption."

Emili nodded, impressed. "So, the frameworks essentially served as a roadmap for both offensive and defensive strategies."

Soham chuckled. "Precisely! It is like a chess game. We use industry standards like ISO 27001 to establish a baseline security posture, then leverage MITRE ATT&CK and NIST frameworks to constantly test and refine it. Tools like MITRE ATT&CK Navigator and NIST Cybersecurity Framework tools help us map threats to controls, prioritize investments, and track our progress."

Emili, her brow furrowed slightly, contemplated. "But surely implementing and maintaining such an integrated approach is not without its challenges?"

Soham acknowledged the hurdle. "Integration is one hurdle. Different frameworks use their own terminology and methodologies, requiring a skilled team to bridge the gap. Additionally, keeping pace with the evolving threat landscape demands continuous adaptation and resource investment. But the benefits outweigh the challenges. The data-driven approach helps us prioritize effectively, allocate resources efficiently, and build a truly resilient cybersecurity posture."

The sunlight streaming through the window seemed to shimmer with the energy of their exchange. This conversation had transcended a simple interview, becoming a testament to the power of knowledge, frameworks, and proactive defense in the ever-evolving realm of cybersecurity.

"Soham, your insights on framework integration are fascinating. But the threat landscape varies across industries. How do you adapt your approach to address industry-specific challenges?"

Soham, invigorated by her question, replied, "Precisely, Emili. Take finance, for instance. We layer industry standards like PCI DSS over the NIST and MITRE frameworks. PCI DSS mandates specific controls for credit card data protection, so we map relevant ATT&CK techniques like web skimming and malware injection to those controls. This ensures our Blue Team prioritizes measures like intrusion detection and vulnerability scanning to safeguard sensitive financial data."

Emili, intrigued, nodded. "And what about other industries? How do they address such unique threats?"

Soham chuckled. "Healthcare is another prime example. With the rise of ransomware attacks targeting hospitals, we heavily emphasize data backup and recovery alongside NIST and ATT&CK integration. Additionally, frameworks like HIPAA guide our control selection, prioritizing measures like access control and encryption to protect patient privacy."

Emili, her brow furrowing slightly, pondered further. "But surely complying with multiple frameworks can be complicated."

Soham acknowledged the challenge. "It is a precarious walk. Striking a balance between industry mandates like DORA in the digital operational resilience space and broader frameworks like ISO 27001 can be tricky. The key lies in mapping industry-specific controls to the broader framework categories, ensuring comprehensive coverage while adhering to specific regulations."

Emili, impressed by his nuanced approach, pressed on. "So, you essentially tailor your framework integration based on the industry's unique attack landscape and regulatory environment?"

Soham grinned. "Exactly! It is like a security chef, carefully blending different ingredients to create a dish that is both delicious and nutritious. We leverage the strengths of each framework, adapting our approach to address the specific vulnerabilities and threats faced by each industry."

Emili's gaze sharpened with intellectual hunger. "Soham, your framework integration approach demonstrates exceptional thoroughness and attention to detail. But in practical terms, how do you navigate the constant tug-of-war between robust security and smooth operational efficiency, especially in sectors like manufacturing or supply chain management?"

Soham, appreciating her insightful question, leaned back in his chair. "It is a delicate dance. In manufacturing, for instance, stringent security measures can slow down production lines, impacting output and profitability. We constantly strive to find that sweet spot between robust defense and streamlined operations."

Emili, intrigued, leaned forward. "Can you give me an example of how you achieve this balance?"

Soham chuckled. "Certainly. We might implement network segmentation to contain potential breaches within specific manufacturing zones, ensuring overall production is not crippled. Additionally, we leverage DevSecOps principles to integrate security considerations into the software development lifecycle, preventing vulnerabilities from creeping in at the code level."

Emili, impressed by the specific approach, nodded. "Supply chains, with their complex web of interconnected organizations, create fertile ground for vulnerabilities to hide. Is not it?"

Soham's expression turned serious. "Supply chain security is indeed a budding problem. We utilize frameworks like NIST Cybersecurity Supply Chain Risk Management (SCRM) to assess and mitigate risks across our vendor network. This involves collaborating with suppliers to implement secure coding practices, vulnerability management programs, and incident response protocols."

Emili, her brow furrowed slightly, contemplated further. "But certainly, pursuing external entities to emphasize security over efficiency can be challenging?"

Soham acknowledged the hurdle. "Communication and collaboration are key. We educate our vendors about the shared risks, demonstrating how robust security benefits everyone by minimizing disruptions and reputational damage. Additionally, industry-specific standards like NIST SP 800-161 for the supply chain security of controlled unclassified information (CUI) provide a common language and baseline for collaboration."

Emili, impressed by his emphasis on collaboration, pressed on. "So, it's not just about deploying technology, but also fostering a culture of security awareness and shared responsibility amongst different stakeholders?"

Soham grinned. "Absolutely! Technology is just one piece of the puzzle, Emili. Building a truly resilient ecosystem requires continuous learning, open communication, and a shared commitment. Continuous learning ensures cybersecurity teams stay ahead of evolving threats, adapting their skills and knowledge. Open communication fosters collaboration and rapid information sharing, enabling faster detection and response to security incidents. A shared commitment throughout the organization prioritizes security, embedding it within all actions and decisions to create a more resilient defense against cyberattacks. It's an ongoing journey, but one that ultimately leads to a more secure and sustainable future for everyone."

The sunlight filtering through the window seemed to reflect the dynamic nature of their conversation. This interview had transcended a normal interview, becoming a glimpse into the complex interplay of security, efficiency, and collaboration in the face of evolving threats across diverse industries.

III

Navigating the Digital Archipelago: Platforms, Frameworks, and the Elusive Fortress

Sunlight, tinged with the golden hues of afternoon, streamed through the glass walls of the conference room, casting long shadows that danced like phantoms across the table. Here, in this sterile microcosm, a battle of wits unfolded – not with clashing steel, but with the whispered hum of rapid-fire exchange of technical jargon. Emili, her gaze sharp with intellectual curiosity, leaned across the table, a lone explorer navigating the uncharted territories of cybersecurity. Across from her, Soham, a seasoned guardian of the digital realm, parried her inquiries with the confidence of a seasoned strategist.

"Soham," Emili's voice cut through the quiet howl of the air conditioning, "your ability to harmonize frameworks and controls is like conducting a complex symphony, and the result is truly impressive. But the digital landscape is a diverse archipelago, with islands of cloud, containerized landscapes, and SaaS (software as a service) offerings rising from the digital sea. How do your strategies adapt to these different platforms?"

Soham, relishing the shift in conversation, leaned back in his chair, a smile playing on his lips. "That is a crucial frontier. Each platform possesses its own unique topography, presenting distinct challenges and opportunities for the cybersecurity architect. In the cloud, for instance, we navigate by the compass of the Cloud Security Alliance (CSA) guidelines, aligning our controls with their well-charted best practices."

Emili, her brow furrowed slightly, pressed further. "And what about NIST's venerable framework? Does it still hold dominion in this fragmented realm?"

Soham chuckled. "In the vast and sometimes murky digital sea, NIST serves as a guiding star, offering clear direction and reliable information. Its controls and recommendations provide a universal language, a shared map that allows us to adapt our defenses to the specific contours of each platform. For containers, we might prioritize controls from the SC-4 (System and Communication Security) family to ensure proper isolation and resource allocation. Similarly, in SaaS and PaaS environments, we leverage controls like SC-8 (Identity and Access Management) and IA-5 (Security Assessment and

Authorization) to ensure secure access and data governance."

Emili, her eyes gleaming with understanding, nodded. "So, it is not about applying a one-size-fits-all approach, but rather tailoring your defenses based on the specific risks and vulnerabilities inherent to each platform?"

Soham grinned. "Precisely! Each platform is a distinct ecosystem, with its own set of predators and prey. In the cloud, we contend with shared responsibility models and potential data breaches across virtual borders. Containers present challenges with lateral movement and runtime risks. Each platform demands a nuanced understanding of its vulnerabilities and a meticulous selection of controls to mitigate those threats."

The sunlight, now a fiery ember as the day waned, seemed to reflect the intensity of their discussion. This conversation had become a masterclass in the art of adapting cyber defenses to the evolving landscape of platforms and technologies. Soham, a seasoned cartographer, had unveiled the intricate maps and guiding principles that navigate the treacherous waters of the digital archipelago.

Emili leaned forward, her gaze sharpening like a laser focused on a distant target. "Soham, your explanation of platform-specific security paints a clear picture. But the cloud, with its shared responsibility and ephemeral nature, presents unique challenges. Can you elaborate on how you navigate the intricacies of container security within this cloud ecosystem?"

Soham, invigorated by her shift in focus, grinned. "Ah, containers, Emili, miniature fortresses holding precious code, yet vulnerable to subtle breaches in the shared walls. In this realm, we dance a delicate waltz between agility and isolation. NIST's SC-4 family becomes our choreographer, guiding us towards controls like resource quotas and network segmentation to prevent malicious containers from spilling their secrets or commandeering neighboring resources."

Emili, intrigued by the metaphor, nodded. "But is not the ephemeral nature of containers a double-edged sword? They vanish quickly, potentially masking malicious activity."

Soham chuckled. "Indeed, Emili. That is where continuous monitoring and logging become our watchful sentinels. Tools like container runtime security and vulnerability scanners act as vigilant guards, scrutinizing each container's ephemeral life for anomalous behavior or hidden flaws."

Emili, her brow furrowed slightly, pondered further. "And what about data security? How do you ensure sensitive information does not escape the confines of these fleeting containers?"

Soham's expression turned serious. "Data encryption at rest and in transit becomes our sacred shield. We leverage tools like secrets management and key vaults to ensure only authorized processes access sensitive data within the container, even if its ephemeral walls crumble."

"But the cloud's not the only archipelago we navigate," Emili's voice broke the contemplative silence. "Cloud-based services offer convenience, but also pose distinct security concerns. Can you shed light on your approach in these pre-built environments?"

Soham, eager to explore new terrain, readily responded. "Ah, yes, the allure of convenience comes with its own set of risks. In SaaS, we rely heavily on controls like IA-5, scrutinizing the vendor's security posture and data governance practices before entrusting them with our precious data. We leverage penetration testing and threat modeling to identify potential vulnerabilities in the shared infrastructure, ensuring our data isn't caught in the crossfire of another tenant's breach."

Emili, impressed by the proactive approach, pressed on. "And what do you do for PaaS, where applications are built upon their platform? How do you ensure your own code does not introduce vulnerabilities into their secure foundation?"

Soham chuckled. "DevSecOps becomes our guiding mantra. We integrate security considerations into every stage of the software development lifecycle, from secure coding practices to vulnerability scanning and penetration testing. This shared responsibility, where vendor and user security practices intertwine, demands constant vigilance and open communication to build a truly secure fortress on their platform."

The sunlight, a silent observer to their intellectual exchange, seemed to shimmer with the energy of their conversation. This interview had become a masterclass in practical cybersecurity, revealing the dynamic interplay between real-world frameworks and technical expertise in the face of ever-evolving threats.

Emili's eyes gleamed with a newfound determination as she leaned forward. "Soham, your insights into platform-specific security are fascinating. But theory needs teeth, doesn't it? Can you walk me through some specific tools and methodologies you employ in the trenches, across the likes of AWS (Amazon Web Services), Azure, and GCP (Google Cloud Platform)?"

"Emili, your thirst for specifics never ceases to impress," Soham chuckled, leaning back in his chair. "In the AWS realm," Soham continued, "we wield tools like Guard Duty, a watchful sentry constantly scanning for malicious activity across your cloud resources. Imagine it as a tireless bloodhound, sniffing out unusual network traffic or suspicious configuration changes."

"Azure has its own comprehensive security information and event management (SIEM) platform, Sentinel, which acts as a central command center, aggregating logs and alerts from across your Azure environment. Think of it as a seasoned strategist, piecing together clues from disparate sources to identify potential threats."

"And Google Cloud Platform boasts Chronicle," Soham added, "a cloud native SIEM solution that excels at threat hunting and incident response. Picture it as a nimble scout, navigating the vast expanse of your GCP resources to uncover hidden vulnerabilities and track attacker movements."

But, Emili," Soham's voice lowered, "we do not rely solely on these native sentinels. Third-party tools like Palo Alto's Prisma Cloud or MacAfee MVISION Cloud supplement our defenses, offering specialized expertise in areas like container security or workload protection."

"Take containers, for instance," Soham explained. "Investing in robust container security solutions like Sysdig or Aqua Security can provide deep visibility into container operations, empowering proactive threat detection and mitigation. They act like microscopic security cameras, peering into the ephemeral world of containers to detect malware or suspicious processes before they wreak havoc."

"And when it comes to securing workloads across different cloud platforms," Soham added, "tools like CloudSploit or StackRox shine. They bridge the gap between diverse cloud environments, offering centralized policy management and vulnerability scanning, ensuring consistent security across the entire hybrid or multi-cloud landscape."

Emili, her eyes gleaming with understanding, nodded. "So, it is like building a layered defense, Emili, combining native cloud tools with specialized third-party solutions to create a comprehensive security ecosystem tailored to your specific cloud environment and needs."

Soham smiled. "Of course. Remember, in the ever-evolving digital landscape, no single tool holds the key to absolute security. It is the strategic combination of native expertise, third-party specialization, and continuous vigilance that truly fortifies your digital fortress."

"Could you please give me an example"? Emili looked forward to Soham's blazing eyes.

"Well. Let us delve into the annals of successful cloud security implementation. Soham leaned forward, his voice taking on a narrative tone. "In case of an e-commerce company, initially, their security posture resembled a patchwork quilt, each cloud service stitched together with disparate tools and policies. Data breaches loomed like specters, threatening customer trust and brand reputation."

Emili, captivated, leaned in closer. "So, how did they turn the tide?"

Soham chuckled. "They adopted a zero-trust approach, Emili. Imagine erecting a fortified gatehouse around every cloud resource, meticulously verifying each access request before granting entry. Tools like AWS IAM and Azure Active Directory became their digital gatekeepers, enforcing least-privilege access and multi-factor authentication."

"Furthermore," Soham continued, "They embraced cloud-native security solutions like Guard Duty and Sentinel. These vigilant sentinels scanned their cloud environment for anomalies, identifying suspicious activity like unauthorized resource access or unusual data exfiltration attempts before they could escalate into full-blown breaches."

Emili's eyes widened. "And the results?"

Soham grinned. "Their transformation was remarkable. Data breaches became a distant memory, customer trust soared, and their cloud environment hummed with the confident thrum of robust security. They proved that embracing the cloud does not have to be a security gamble, but rather an opportunity to build a more resilient and agile digital fortress."

"Now, let's shift gears," Soham said, his voice softening slightly, "and analyze the case of a well-known university, a prestigious institution facing a different kind of cloud security challenge. Their research data, the lifeblood of academic progress, resided in a cloud labyrinth, accessible to numerous researchers across diverse institutions."

Emili, her brow furrowed, contemplated. "How did they balance security with open collaboration?"

Soham smiled. "They adopted robust data security measures, including advanced DLP (Data Loss Prevention) solutions like Google Cloud DLP and Microsoft Purview. These digital watchdogs scanned research data for sensitive information like personally identifiable data (PII) or intellectual property, alerting administrators to potential leaks before they could occur."

"Furthermore," Soham added, "The university embraced granular access controls using federated authentication and containerized environments. Imagine each research project as a secure island within the cloud, accessible only to authorized personnel and shielded from unauthorized intrusion."

Emili nodded, impressed. "So, they carefully navigated the trade-off between robust security and open communication, ensuring sensitive data remained protected while facilitating the vital exchange of knowledge."

Soham smiled. "Indeed, moving beyond the fallacy of unbreachable barriers, they championed cloud security as a cooperative effort, secured by powerful technology and rigorous measures."

The sunlight, now a soft twilight glow, seemed to reflect the shifting focus of their conversation. This dialogue had delved into the intricate world of container security, revealing the delicate dance between agility, isolation, and the persistent threat of unseen adversaries lurking within the ephemeral walls. "Soham," Emili's voice shattered the hushed stillness, "your case studies were fascinating. Diving deeper into the university's approach particularly piqued my curiosity. How did they manage to foster a culture of secure collaboration within the cloud, where data protection and knowledge sharing coexist?"

Soham, relishing the shift in focus, leaned back in his chair, a thoughtful smile playing on his lips. Emili, you are right. Addressing the human side is paramount for achieving effective cloud security. Technology is undeniably crucial, but without a culture of security awareness and collaboration, even the most sophisticated tools remain inert sentinels."

He continued, his voice morphed, "The university understood this well. They embarked on a comprehensive security awareness program, educating researchers and administrators alike about the potential risks and best practices for secure cloud collaboration. Data classification workshops helped everyone understand the sensitivity of different information, while role-based training equipped personnel with the knowledge and tools to handle their data responsibly."

"Furthermore," Soham added, "They fostered a culture of shared responsibility. Researchers, administrators, and IT (Information Technology) teams collaborated closely, forming a united front against potential threats. Incident response drills not only tested their technical defenses but also strengthened communication and coordination channels, ensuring a swift and efficient response to any security breach."

Emili, her brow furrowed slightly, pondered further. "Prioritizing security can feel like a burden for researchers already focused on achieving their research goals."

Soham chuckled. "Indeed. They addressed this by highlighting the benefits of robust security. They demonstrated how secure data practices not only protect against breaches but also enhance research integrity and build trust with collaborators and funding agencies."

"Ultimately," Soham concluded, "their success stemmed from their holistic approach. They combined cutting-edge technology with a comprehensive security awareness program and a culture of shared responsibility. They proved that cloud security is not just about technical prowess, but also about fostering a collaborative mindset where everyone recognizes their role in safeguarding sensitive information and enabling secure knowledge exchange."

The twilight had surrendered to the velvety embrace of night, the cityscape twinkling outside the window like a constellation of challenges and opportunities. This conversation had unveiled the multifaceted nature of platform-specific security, revealing the unique strategies and considerations required to navigate the cloud, containerized environments, and managed platforms in the ever-evolving digital archipelago. This dialogue explored the triumphs of successful cloud security implementations, offering practical insights and inspiration for navigating the ever-evolving digital landscape with confidence and resilience.

"Soham," Emili's gaze sharpened, a hint of technical curiosity lighting her eyes, "the secure research environment description was truly compelling. I am particularly intrigued by their granular access controls. Can you elaborate on the technical underpinnings of this system, and how it aligns with industry best practices like ISO 27001 or the NIST Cybersecurity Framework?"

Soham, relishing the opportunity to delve deeper, grinned. "Ah, you've touched upon the nerve center of their secure collaboration. They leveraged a combination of technologies and best practices to achieve their granular access goals. Imagine a layered fortress, each layer adding another ring of defense."

"At the foundation," Soham continued, "lay role-based access control (RBAC) aligned with ISO 27001's Annex A controls. Researchers were assigned specific roles with predefined permissions, ensuring access only to data and resources relevant to their projects. Think of it as granting each researcher a unique key, opening just the specific doors they need for their research, and no more."

"But wait," Emili interjected, a thoughtful crease appearing on her forehead, "would not static RBAC limit collaboration and hinder research progress?"

Soham chuckled. "The need for more fine-grained access control beyond roles and permissions in RBAC led them to layer ABAC on top, enabling them to enforce access based on dynamic attributes. Imagine each data asset tagged with specific attributes – sensitivity level, project affiliation, research methodology. ABAC dynamically evaluated these attributes against a researcher's profile, granting access only if their attributes matched the data's requirements."

"This dynamic duo," Soham elaborated, "adheres to the NIST Cybersecurity Framework's principle of least privilege, ensuring minimum necessary access while enabling flexible collaboration. Researchers could still collaborate on projects within their authorized parameters, but unauthorized access attempts were met with a firm digital 'no trespassing' sign."

Emili, her eyes gleaming with understanding, nodded. "So, it is like a dynamic puzzle, constantly adjusting access based on changing research needs and data attributes?"

Soham grinned. "Exactly! And to further bolster their defenses, the university implemented continuous monitoring and logging across their cloud environment. Tools aligned with CIS (Centre of Information Security) Benchmarks tracked user activity and data access, providing real-time insights and alerting administrators to any suspicious behavior, adhering to the MITRE ATT&CK framework's focus on proactive threat detection."

"Furthermore," Soham added, "their security policies, meticulously documented and reviewed periodically, enshrined these best practices into their organizational DNA. Think of it as a blueprint for secure collaboration, constantly updated to reflect evolving threats and research needs."

Emili, impressed by the intricate layering of technology and best practices, leaned forward. "So, the cultural shift towards secure collaboration was not just about awareness, but also about embedding these principles into the very fabric of their cloud infrastructure and policies?"

Soham chuckled. "You have grasped the essence, Emili! They understood that true security is a holistic endeavor, where technology, best practices, and culture intertwine to form an impregnable fortress. Unified success unlocks secure, collaborative cloud research. Imagine secure, collaborative research in the cloud - their success makes it a reality."

Emili's gaze remained fixed on Soham, the technical curiosity in her eyes burning brighter than ever. "Your explanation of access controls unlocked a whole new understanding for me, Soham. But their success hinges not just on who can access what, but also on how they monitor and respond to potential threats. Can you shed light on their continuous monitoring and logging practices? How do they ensure they are catching anomalies before they turn into full-blown breaches?"

Soham, invigorated by her shift in focus, leaned forward, a knowing smile playing on his lips. "Ah, Emili, a vast digital tapestry extends beyond the university, woven from vigilant threads. Each thread, a watchful eye scanning for threats, its observations composing a real-time narrative of security." "At the heart of this operation," Soham continued, "throbbed a combination of cloud-native security information and event management (SIEM) solutions like Google Cloud Chronicle and third-party tools aligned with the Cloud Security Alliance (CSA) CloudTrail best practices. These digital bloodhounds relentlessly analyze logs from across their cloud infrastructure, searching for unusual network traffic, unauthorized access attempts, or suspicious data exfiltration patterns."

Emili, her brow furrowed slightly, pondered further. "But with such a vast amount of data, is not it difficult to identify the truly concerning needles in the haystack?"

Soham chuckled. "Indeed. This is where sophisticated threat intelligence and SOAR platforms step in to empower your security team with deeper insights and faster responses, keeping you ahead of attackers. It is needed to leverage tools like MITRE ATT&CK Navigator and threat feeds aligned with NIST Cybersecurity Framework recommendations to prioritize alerts based on known attack patterns and attacker tactics, techniques, and procedures (TTPs)."

"Furthermore," Soham added, "their incident response strategy resembled a well-rehearsed play. The university teams trained in accordance with ISO 27002 best practices had clearly defined roles and responsibilities, ensuring swift and coordinated action upon any alert. Imagine a digital fire brigade, each member knowing their role and working in unison to contain and extinguish any potential security fire."

Emili, impressed by the meticulousness of their approach, nodded. "So, continuous monitoring is not just about collecting data, but also about analyzing it intelligently and responding promptly to potential threats?"

Soham grinned. "Precisely, Emili! Prevention is crucial, but effective incident response is equally pivotal. Their layered approach, combining vigilant monitoring, intelligent analysis, and rapid response, ensured that even the most cunning attackers would face a formidable digital fortress." Adjusting his glasses as he leaned forward, continued. "Let's dissect the intricate dance between vigilant monitoring and rapid response that safeguards university's research haven."

He described how their chosen SIEM solutions were not mere data repositories, but intelligent analysts. Tools like Chronicle leveraged machine learning algorithms, trained on vast datasets of known attack patterns and threat profiles, to sniff out anomalies like bloodhounds on the scent of danger.

"Human direction remains crucial, even for advanced algorithms," Soham added. "They fed their SIEMs (Security Information and Event Management) curated threat intelligence feeds aligned with MITRE ATT&CK frameworks. Imagine these feeds as detailed maps of attacker tactics, guiding the SIEMs to prioritize alerts based on the likelihood of a real attack."

Emili, her eyes gleaming with curiosity, pressed on. "And what happens when an alert is triggered?"

Soham's voice lowered as he described the well-oiled machinery of their incident response. "Think of it as a digital SWAT team springing into action. Pre-defined playbooks, adhering to ISO 27002 best practices, dictated the response for each type of alert. Containment protocols kicked in, isolating potentially compromised systems to prevent further damage."

"Meanwhile," Soham continued, "dedicated incident responders, trained in simulated drills and armed with SOAR platforms, investigated the alert's origin and scope.

"Soham," Emili's voice cut through the quiet hum, a hint of investigative zeal in her eyes, "your description of the university's incident response was truly impressive. But in the heat of the moment, clear and efficient communication is crucial. Can you elaborate on their communication channels and protocols during an incident response? How do they ensure everyone is on the same page and the response remains coordinated?"

Soham, relishing the opportunity to delve deeper, leaned back in his chair, a knowing smile playing on his lips. "In effective incident response, seamless communication acts as the central nervous system, ensuring coordinated action despite the whirlwind of activity."

He explained how organizations prioritized internal communication channels like secure instant messaging platforms and dedicated incident response channels within their collaboration tools. These channels, adhering to ISO 27002 best practices for incident communication, ensured immediate and secure information exchange between all stakeholders, from technical responders to senior leadership.

"But it does not stop there," Soham continued. "Engaging with stakeholders outside the organization is also essential. They established clear protocols for notifying regulatory bodies and affected researchers, balancing transparency with the need to protect sensitive information and ongoing investigations."

Emili, her brow furrowed slightly, pondered further. "And what about post-incident analysis? How do organizations ensure they learn from each incident and improve their defenses?"

Soham chuckled. "As the proverb goes - 'learn from your mistakes.' After every incident, conduct thorough post-mortems, meticulously review logs, response actions, and engage stakeholders through pre-established communication channels. Imagine accurately dissecting the digital battlefield, identifying weaknesses and areas for improvement."

"These post-mortems," Soham added, "fed directly into their continuous improvement cycle. Identified vulnerabilities were patched, playbooks were updated, and training exercises were revised to address the specific tactics employed in the attack. Consider it a self-protecting ecosystem, proactively adapting to survive in a dynamic environment."

Emili, impressed by their thorough approach, nodded. "So, communication is not just about reacting to an incident, but also about learning and evolving to prevent future attacks?"

Soham grinned. "Precisely. Incident response is a continuous loop, not a one-time event. By prioritizing clear communication, meticulous post-mortems, and continuous improvement, any company can ensure that every incident, however challenging, ultimately made their digital fortress even stronger."

"Soham," Emili's voice ripped through the tranquil hum of the room, a hint of practicality lacing her tone, "your insights into the university's security measures have been truly illuminating. But with such a complex and dynamic environment, how do they ensure clear ownership and accountability across all their security operations and incident response activities?"

Soham, impressed by her astute question, grinned. "Ah, Emili, you hit the nail on the head! Organizations leverage a comprehensive RACI (Responsible, Accountable, Consulted, Informed) matrix to orchestrate their security operations and incident response like a well-oiled machine."

He explained how each stage of their security operations, from access control configuration to vulnerability patching, had clearly defined roles mapped out in the RACI matrix. The "Responsible" party owned the task execution, the "Accountable" individual ensured successful completion, while the "Consulted" stakeholders provided expertise and guidance, and the "Informed" personnel stayed updated on progress and potential risks.

Emili, her brow furrowed slightly, pondered further. "And during an incident response scenario, how does the

RACI matrix adapt to ensure swift and coordinated action?"

Soham chuckled. "Their RACI matrix transforms into a dynamic battlefield map during an incident. Incident responders, pre-assigned as "Responsible" for specific tasks based on their skillsets, take the lead, while the "Accountable" incident commander orchestrates the overall response. Meanwhile, relevant experts and leadership remain "Consulted" for critical decisions, and all stakeholders are kept "Informed" through secure communication channels."

"This dynamic RACI approach," Soham added, "eliminates confusion and finger-pointing, ensuring everyone knows their role and can execute it effectively under pressure. Think of it as a digital fire team, each member trained and equipped to handle their specific task, ultimately working together to extinguish the security threat."

Emili, impressed by the adaptable nature of their RACI matrix, nodded. "So, it is not just about static roles, but about a flexible framework that adapts to the demands of the situation, ensuring everyone contributes to the best of their abilities?"

Soham grinned. "Precisely, Emili! They understood that clear ownership and accountability are crucial for effective security. Their dynamic RACI matrix serves as the invisible conductor, harmonizing the efforts of their security team and ensuring a swift and coordinated response to any threat, no matter how complex."

Emili leaned forward, her eyes alight with curiosity. "Soham, your explanation of the RACI matrix has intrigued me. I understand its importance in streamlining operations, but how do they translate those abstract roles into concrete responsibilities for different security tasks? Is there a specific methodology they use to define who does what?"

Soham, relishing the opportunity to delve deeper, chuckled. "Of course. No one should rely on guesswork. Every company shall employ a meticulous process rooted in industry best practices and tailored to their specific cloud environment."

He outlined their approach, explaining how they began by mapping out the entire security workflow, from proactive tasks like access control configuration and vulnerability management to reactive activities like incident response and threat hunting. Each stage of this workflow was then broken down into granular tasks, ensuring no crucial step got overlooked.

"Next," Soham continued, "came the crucial stage of role definition. Organizations in general leverage frameworks like NIST SP 800-161 and tailored them to their specific cloud platform. This provided a solid foundation for identifying the roles needed for each security task, considering factors like skillsets, workload distribution, and potential conflicts of interest."

Emili, her brow crumpled slightly, pondered further. "And how do they ensure everyone on the team understands their RACI assignments? Is it just documented somewhere, or do they employ specific communication strategies?"

Soham chuckled. "Clarity is key to RACI success. No one leaves assignments to chance. RACI matrix is a living document, readily accessible to everyone involved. Additionally, organizations conduct regular training sessions to ensure everyone understands their roles and responsibilities, both in general and for specific scenarios."

"Furthermore," Soham added, "they leverage collaborative tools and communication channels to foster transparency and accountability. Team members can easily access the RACI matrix, discuss task ownership, and raise concerns if any ambiguities arise. This open communication loop ensures everyone is on the same page and can effectively fulfil their role within the security orchestra."

Emili, impressed by their meticulous approach, nodded. "So, it's not just about assigning roles, but about creating a framework for understanding, communication, and continuous improvement?"

Soham grinned. "Precisely! In fact, everyone should recognize that the RACI matrix is only as effective as its implementation. By meticulously defining roles, ensuring clear communication, and fostering a culture of collaboration, they turn this framework into a powerful tool for streamlined security operations and agile incident response."

Imagine them piecing together a digital puzzle, analyzing logs and forensic data to identify the attacker's TTPs and mitigate the threat."

Emili, impressed by the coordinated response, nodded. "So, it is not just about technology, but also about having the right people and processes in place?"

Soham grinned. "Absolutely. Even the most robust tools are useless without skilled humans interpreting the data and taking decisive action. Therefore, investment in training and incident response preparedness is indispensable to ensure that every alert was met with a swift and coordinated counteroffensive."

The moonlight, now a silvery halo framing the cityscape, mirrored the meticulous nature of their discussion. This conversation had delved into the specific aspects of Ivy University's RACI matrix implementation, revealing their process for defining roles, communicating assignments, and fostering a culture of understanding and collaboration, transforming the RACI matrix into a cornerstone of their robust cloud security posture.

• 41 •

IV

Beyond the Breach: Minimizing the Blast Radius

The clock ticks past six o 'clock, casting long shadows across the expansive interview hall. Moonlight streamed through the panoramic windows, bathing the sterile white space in an ethereal glow. Emili and Soham sat perched on sleek, ergonomic chairs, their conversation weaving intricate tapestries of security paradigm.

The air crackled with intellectual energy, fueled by Emili's insatiable curiosity and Soham's deep reservoir of technical expertise. Their dialogue had traversed the granular realm of access controls, the vigilant watch of continuous monitoring, and the well-oiled machinery of incident response. Now, Emili's gaze held a glint of future-gazing, as she leaned forward, her voice echoing in the vast hall.

"Soham," she began, "we have delved deep into the university's impressive security measures, including their incident response strategies. However, I was wondering if any futuristic measures like zero trust framework or artificial intelligence would help to strengthen cyber security and incident response. Can you shed some light in this respect?

Soham, a hint of a smile playing on his lips, relished the opportunity to unveil the practical benefits of adopting a forward-thinking approach like zero trust. He adjusted his glasses, the moonlight catching the glint of anticipation in his eyes.

"Ah, that is the very crux of zero-trust's appeal," he began, his voice resonating with conviction. "Think of a traditional castle, with a single fortified gate guarding the entire domain. A breach at that gate grants unfettered access to everything within. Now, imagine any organization as a sprawling metropolis, each building secured by its own robust defenses, with access granted only on a need-to-know basis."

He paused, his tone acquired a captivating lilt, before continuing. "In a zero-trust realm, even if an attacker breaches one outer layer, they are met with a labyrinth of fortified checkpoints. Each system scrutinizes their credentials, each access request is evaluated dynamically, and lateral movement becomes a near-impossible feat. This segmentation, this granular control over access, significantly limits the blast radius of any potential incident."

Emili, her brow furrowed in thought, interjected, "So, it is like building a series of firewalls within the digital walls themselves, preventing a small spark from erupting into an uncontrollable inferno?"

Soham chuckled, his eyes twinkling. "Precisely, by actively implementing zero trust principles, organizations can build a more resilient digital environment where every access attempt is scrutinized, and lateral movement is restricted. Even if an attacker enters, their options are severely limited, their ability to steal data or disrupt operations significantly curtailed. This, in essence, is the true power of zero-trust – it minimizes the impact of the inevitable, ensuring that even in the face of adversity, organization's cyber landscape remains secure."

The moonlight, now a gentle symphony on the city skyline, seemed to echo the thoughtful silence that had settled in the interview hall. Emili, her gaze fixed on Soham, leaned forward, her curiosity etched on her features.

"Soham," she began, her voice laced with intrigue, "your explanation of zero-trust has been truly illuminating. But implementing such a radical shift in security posture would not be without its challenges. Can you shed light on the hurdles organizations typically face when embarking on this zero-trust journey?"

Soham, a knowing smile playing on his lips, relished the opportunity to delve deeper. "Ah, Emili, you cracked the code," he chuckled. "Zero-trust, while undeniably powerful, is not a magic spell cast upon existing infrastructure. It is a transformative journey, and like any journey, it is littered with its fair share of obstacles."

He paused, allowing the weight of his words to sink in before elaborating. "One of the first, and perhaps most daunting, challenges is legacy systems. Many organizations, Ivy University included, have a treasure trove of legacy applications and infrastructure, often woven into the very fabric of their operations. Integrating these disparate systems into a zero-trust architecture can be a complex and time-consuming endeavor."

Emili, her brow furrowed slightly, interjected. "So, it is like trying to retrofit a modern security system into an ancient castle? The foundation might not always be built for the new technology."

Soham chuckled. "Exactly, Emili! And then there is the issue of user experience. Zero-trust often necessitates stricter access controls and authentication protocols, which, if not implemented thoughtfully, can disrupt workflows and hinder user productivity. Security and usability are two sides of the same coin; prioritizing one over the other hinders adoption. Gaining users' trust requires robust security measures that are still user-friendly."

"Furthermore," Soham added, "organizational culture plays an important role. Zero-trust demands a shift in mindset, from perimeter-based defense to continuous micro-monitoring. Employees need to be onboard with the philosophy, understand their roles within the new security paradigm, and adapt to potentially stricter access protocols."

Emili, her eyes gleaming with renewed curiosity, pressed on. "And what about skills and resources? Implementing zero-trust often requires specialized expertise and tools. Does this pose a significant hurdle for organizations, particularly smaller ones?"

Soham nodded. "Indeed. The talent pool for skilled zero-trust architects and engineers is still maturing, and the cost of acquiring the necessary tools and technologies can be substantial. This can be a significant challenge for smaller organizations with limited resources."

As the final words faded, a contemplative silence descended upon the hall. The moonlight, now a silent observer, seemed to acknowledge the complexities inherent in the zero-trust journey. This conversation had revealed the challenges organizations face when embarking on this transformative approach, from legacy systems and user experience to cultural shifts and resource constraints.

But Soham's eyes, even in the muted moonlight, held a glint of unwavering conviction. "Despite the challenges," he began, his voice resonating with optimism, "the benefits of zero-trust are undeniable. It offers a future-proof security posture, enhanced resilience against cyber threats, and a granular control over access that was unimaginable just a few years ago." Emili, her gaze mirroring his conviction, nodded resolutely.

The moonlight, a silvery sheen across the cityscape, seemed to hold its breath as Emili leaned forward, her gaze laser-focused on Soham. "Your insights into zero-trust have been nothing short of fascinating," she began, her voice laced with intellectual hunger. "While the weeds of implementation obscure the view, I yearn to glimpse the seed at its root. What, at its most fundamental level, is the underlying principle that drives this transformative security approach?"

Soham, a hint of a smile playing on his lips, relished the opportunity to delve into the philosophical heart of zero-trust. "Ah, Emili," he chuckled, "you have reached for the very root of the digital fortress. The bedrock upon which zero-trust is built is a simple, yet profound, principle: never trust, always verify."

He paused, letting the weight of his words settle before elaborating. "In the traditional castle analogy, we assume everyone within the walls is friendly, trusting them to roam freely. Zero-trust flips this paradigm on its head. Every access request, every user, every device, is treated with healthy skepticism. Building trust in sensitive systems requires continuous verification and granular access controls to safeguard data and privacy."

Emili, her brow furrowed in thought, interjected. "So, it is about constantly questioning assumptions, never taking security for granted, even within the perceived 'safe' confines of your own digital walls?"

Soham chuckled. "Precisely! This constant vigilance, this zero-tolerance for implicit trust, is what makes zero-trust so powerful. It dismantles the very idea of a secure perimeter, recognizing that vulnerabilities can lurk anywhere, even within trusted systems. By continuously verifying and authorizing every interaction, zero-trust significantly reduces the attack surface and minimizes the damage potential of any potential breach."

"Think of it," Soham continued, his voice animated, "as a layered onion. Each layer represents a verification checkpoint, peeling away assumptions and granting access only to those who pass every test. This layered approach, this fundamental distrust in the face of potential threats, is the essence of zero-trust."

Emili, her eyes gleaming with newfound understanding, nodded thoughtfully. "So, it is not just about technology or tools, but about a fundamental shift in security mindset, a constant questioning and verification that keeps even the most sophisticated attackers at bay."

Soham grinned. "Zero-trust is not just a technological marvel, but a philosophical revolution in the way we approach security. It is about embracing the inherent uncertainty of the digital landscape and building defenses that remain vigilant, adaptable, and ultimately, unshakeable."

As the silence settled, the moonlight echoed their dialogue, its soft glow reflecting the profound shift in perspective. This conversation had delved into the very core of zero-trust, revealing the fundamental principle of "never trust, always verify" as the driving force behind this transformative security approach.

The moon, now a celestial spotlight illuminating the interview hall, seemed to hold its breath as Emili leaned forward, her gaze unwavering in its pursuit of knowledge. "Soham," she began, her voice laced with intellectual intrigue, "your delineation of the 'never trust, always verify' principle at the heart of zero-trust has been truly enlightening. But I am curious, how does this translate into concrete mechanisms? What are the specific tools and techniques employed to verify trust and control access within a zero-trust architecture?"

Soham, a knowing smile playing on his lips, relished the opportunity to unveil the intricate mechanics of zero-trust verification. A hush fell over the room as his voice took on a captivating narrative quality. "You have unlocked the hidden pulse of the digital labyrinth. The cornerstone of zero-trust verification lies in a dynamic duo; identity and access management (IAM) principles working in tandem with robust multi-factor authentication (MFA) techniques."

He paused, allowing the weight of his words to sink in before elaborating. "IAM forms the foundation, meticulously mapping and verifying the identities of users, devices, and applications seeking access. Think of it as a digital passport control, scrutinizing every credential presented and granting access only to those deemed authorized."

Emili, her brow furrowed slightly, interpolated. "So, it's about establishing who is who in the digital landscape, ensuring everyone operates under their true digital identities?"

Soham chuckled. "Precisely! But verification goes beyond simply knowing who someone is. MFA adds another layer of security, demanding something you have (like a one-time code) and something you are (like a fingerprint) before granting access. Think of it as a double-layered lock on the digital door, ensuring even if one key is compromised, the second barrier remains."

"Furthermore," Soham added, "zero-trust verification extends beyond initial logins. Continuous monitoring and dynamic authorization techniques scrutinize user behavior and system activity in real-time. Any anomalies, any suspicious deviations from established patterns, trigger immediate scrutiny and potential access revocation. It is like having a vigilant digital security guard patrolling the corridors, constantly questioning and verifying the legitimacy of everyone's movements."

Emili, her eyes gleaming with renewed comprehension, pressed on. "So, it is a multi-layered approach, a continuous dance between verifying identities, activities, and behavior, ensuring no unauthorized entity slips through the cracks?"

Soham nodded. "Indeed! But implementing this symphony of verification is not without its challenges. Integrating disparate IAM systems, managing the complexities of MFA across diverse devices, and striking the right balance between security and user experience are some of the hurdle's organizations face when embarking on this zero-trust journey."

The moonlight, as if mirroring the contemplative mood, cast long shadows across the hall. This conversation had delved into the specific mechanisms of zero-trust verification, revealing the crucial role of IAM and MFA, the continuous monitoring techniques, and the challenges of implementing such a multifaceted approach in real-world scenarios.

The moon, now a silent sentinel against the darkening cityscape, seemed to hold its breath as Emili leaned forward, her gaze unwavering. "Soham," she began, her voice laced with practical curiosity, "your explanation of zero-trust verification mechanisms has been truly illuminating. But theory without practice is merely ink on parchment. How do organizations then navigate the real-world hurdles of integrating diverse IAM systems? Managing a tapestry of MFA implementations and ensuring a seamless user experience?

Soham, a hint of challenge in his eyes, relished the opportunity to delve into the practical trenches. "Ah, Emili," he chuckled, "you have reached the battlefield where theory meets reality. Overcoming these hurdles requires a strategic blend of technology, planning, and a dash of user empathy."

He unfolded his arms, his voice taking on a confident tone. "IAM integration is all about building bridges. Standardized protocols and APIs (Application Programming Interfaces) like OAuth and OpenID Connect act as interpreters, enabling smooth communication between different identity systems, whether it is your on-premises Active Directory or a cloud-based provider. This approach fosters connections and breaks down silos, ensuring a more harmonious identity landscape."

Emili, her brow furrowed in thought, interjected. "So, it is' about establishing a unified approach to identity verification, one that everyone can agree on and implement."

Soham grinned. "Precisely! But IAM integration is just the first step. The MFA orchestra requires a conductor, a centralized platform that manages and orchestrates diverse authentication methods across devices. Biometric scanners, one-time passcodes, and hardware tokens – each instrument plays its own role in the security symphony."

"However," Soham cautioned, "a cacophony of MFA options can overwhelm users. Striking the right balance is crucial. Context-aware MFA, adapting to user risk profiles and access requests, can simplify the experience for low-risk scenarios while deploying stronger measures for high-value assets."

Emili, her eyes gleaming with understanding, pressed on. "So, it is about tailoring the security measures to the situation, ensuring a frictionless experience for routine tasks while keeping the gates firmly shut for critical access points?"

Soham nodded. "Indeed, Emili! And user experience, while often seen as the enemy of security, can be its silent ally. Intuitive interfaces, clear communication about security protocols, and even gamified authentication methods can boost user buy-in and compliance, reducing friction without compromising security."

The moonlight, now a gentle symphony on the city skyline, seemed to hum with anticipation as if acknowledging the importance of user engagement, cast a softer glow upon the hall. This conversation had delved into the practical strategies for navigating the zero-trust battlefield, revealing the importance of standardized IAM integration, centralized MFA management, context-aware authentication, and user-centric security practices. A melody amidst the silence, Emili's voice filled the air. "Soham," she began, her voice brimming with curiosity, "your insights into the practicalities of zero-trust verification have been invaluable. But let us delve deeper.

What tools and technologies form the technological toolbox for these intricate IAM integrations and diverse MFA implementations?"

Soham, a knowing smile playing on his lips, relished the opportunity to unveil the digital arsenal. "You've reached the armory of the digital fortress. When it comes to IAM integration, open-source frameworks like Keycloak and ForgeRock Identity Platform act as the Rosetta Stones, translating the dialects of disparate systems into a common language of identity."

Soham paused. Leaning forward, he began his account, his words imbued with the weight of recollection. "For centralized MFA management, platforms like Duo Security and Ping Identity offer unified dashboards, orchestrating the symphony of authentication methods across devices and applications. Think of them as the maestros of the security orchestra, ensuring each instrument plays its part in perfect harmony."

Emili, her brow furrowed slightly, interjected. "So, these tools act as bridges and conductors, streamlining communication and ensuring a cohesive approach to IAM and MFA across the digital landscape?"

"Precisely! Emili," Soham spoke with a newfound cadence. "But tools alone do not win battles. Let us turn to the real-world trenches, where success stories illuminate the path forward. Take an example of a multinational corporation grappling with legacy systems and diverse cloud environments. By leveraging open-source IAM frameworks and a centralized MFA platform, they can seamlessly integrate their disparate systems, reducing access silos and streamlining user authentication."

Emili, her eyes gleaming with understanding, pressed on. "So, it is not just about the technology, but the strategy behind its implementation."

Soham nodded. "Indeed! Embracing open-source tools and centralized management paves the way for a successful zero-trust journey. And the future of user experience within this fortress holds exciting possibilities. Biometric authentication, like facial recognition and voice analysis, promises a seamless yet secure access experience. Imagine walking into your office and being recognized instantly, no passwords or tokens required."

Emili, her gaze captivated, envisioned the future. "A world where security adapts to our natural interactions, eliminating friction while maintaining robust defenses. It's a fascinating prospect."

Soham grinned. "Zero-trust is not just about technology; it is about reimagining the relationship between security and user experience. By embracing innovation and prioritizing usability, we can build digital fortresses that are not only impregnable but also welcoming to those who reside within."

As the final words faded, the moonlight echoed their dialogue, its soft glow reflecting the transformative potential of zero-trust. This conversation had delved into the technological toolbox, displayed real-world success stories, and unveiled the intriguing future of user experience within this paradigm.

The moonlight, now a luminous tapestry across the cityscape, seemed to hold its breath as Emili leaned forward, her gaze reflecting the twin flames of pragmatism and introspection. "Soham," she began, her voice a blend of intellectual hunger and ethical concern, "your insights into zero-trust have been a revelation. We have explored the tools, witnessed triumphs, and glimpsed the future through the user's lens. But let us delve deeper still. Let us dissect the challenges these organizations faced, glean the lessons learned, and embark on a philosophical discussion about the ethical considerations inherent in this user-centric approach."

Soham, a hint of admiration in his eyes, relished the opportunity to navigate these nuanced terrains. "Ah, Emili," he giggled, "your exploration has led you to the concealed nooks of the digital labyrinth, where triumphs are forged in the fires of adversity and ethics dance with the pragmatism of security."

He paused, letting the weight of her words settle before elaborating. "Consider any healthcare provider implementing their zero-trust security strategy. Integrating legacy medical systems with modern cloud infrastructure proved a Herculean task. User resistance to stricter MFA protocols, particularly for clinicians on the move, threatened to derail the entire process."

Emili, her brow furrowed in thought, interjected. "So, success could not be guaranteed even with the right tools. A company might encounter the human factor, the challenge of adapting to new workflows and convincing end-users to embrace the change."

Soham nodded. "Precisely! But their triumph lay in addressing these challenges head-on. They adopted phased rollouts, prioritized user education and training, and even gamified MFA adoption, turning it into a badge of security honour. The lesson learned? Users buy-in is paramount, and success hinges on finding the sweet spot between robust security and seamless user experience."

Emili, her eyes gleaming with understanding, pressed on. "But user-centricity raises ethical considerations. Biometric authentication, while convenient, raises concerns about privacy and potential misuse. How do we balance security with individual rights in this brave new world?"

Soham chuckled. "Indeed, Emili, you have reached the crux of the matter. Transparency and user control become paramount. Organizations must clearly communicate why specific data is collected and how it is used, while offering options for opting out of certain authentication methods. It is a delicate dance, but one that must be navigated with utmost transparency and ethical responsibility."

As the final words faded, the moonlight bathed the hall in a contemplative glow. This conversation had delved into the triumphs and tribulations of organizational journeys, revealing the challenges of user adoption and the lessons learned in bridging the gap between security and usability.

The moon, now a celestial spotlight dancing across the interview hall, seemed to hold its breath as Emili leaned forward, her gaze as sharp as a laser. "Soham," she began, her voice laced with both intellectual intrigue and ethical concern, "we have delved into the practicalities of zero-trust implementation, witnessing triumphs and learning valuable lessons. But now, let us venture into the ethical minefield. Biometrics, user data, and user-centricity – these hold immense promise, but also raise profound questions. Let us dissect the ethical dilemmas inherent in this brave new world."

Soham, a hint of challenge in his eyes, met her gaze with unwavering curiosity. "You have just touched the philosophical fault lines of the digital fortress." With each detail, his words took on a mesmerizing rhythm, drawing Emili deeper into his enthralling exposition. "Here, security and ethics grapple, and the path forward demands careful consideration. Take the issue of biometrics. Facial recognition, while offering seamless access, can also be misused for mass surveillance. How do we ensure such powerful tools are used for good, not turned into instruments of oppression?"

Emili, her brow crumpled in thought, exclaimed. "And what about user data, the very lifeblood of zero-trust verification? How do we balance the need for granular access control with individual privacy rights? Can we truly offer zero trust without sacrificing some degree of privacy?"

Soham nodded. "Precisely, Emili! These are the questions that keep ethical philosophers and security experts up at night. But let us not forget the real-world heroes navigating these murky waters. Take the example of a financial institution implementing zero-trust. They prioritized user control, offering granular options for biometrics usage and anonymizing collected data wherever possible. They understood that trust in zero-trust hinges on transparency and user empowerment."

Emili, her eyes gleaming with understanding, pressed on. "So, it is not just about the technology, but the ethical principles embedded within its implementation. They chose transparency and user control as their guiding stars."

Soham grinned. "Indeed! But the ethical landscape is not solely shaped by individual organizations. Governance and regulation play a crucial role. Take the nascent laws on biometric usage and data privacy regulations. These act as guardrails, ensuring responsible implementation and safeguarding individual rights within the zero-trust paradigm."

"Furthermore," Soham added, "industry standards and ethical frameworks, like the NIST Privacy Framework, offer invaluable guidance. They provide organizations with a roadmap for navigating the ethical complexities, ensuring their zero-trust journeys are not just secure, but also responsible and respectful of individual rights."

"Soham," she began, her voice laced with an investigative edge, "by examining the ethical considerations embedded within zero-trust practices, we have observed commendable instances of responsible deployment. But I am curious, what forces guide these ethical choices? Are there any industry standards or regulations shaping the future of zero-trust, the guardrails ensuring this powerful technology does not veer into ethical oblivion?"

Soham, a hint of admiration in his eyes, relished the opportunity to navigate these complex terrains. "Ah, Emili," he chuckled, "regulations stand as vigilant sentinels and industry standards act as guiding stars." His voice dipped and soared like a musical scale, painting vivid pictures with each nuance he revealed. "Take the General Data Protection Regulation (GDPR) in Europe, a formidable champion of individual privacy. It sets clear boundaries for data collection, storage, and usage within zero-trust frameworks, demanding transparency and user control over their digital footprints."

Emili, her brow furrowed in thought, interjected. "So, GDPR acts like a digital Bill of Rights, ensuring individuals have a say in how their data is used within security measures?"

Soham nodded. "Precisely, Emili! And across the Atlantic, the California Consumer Privacy Act (CCPA) echoes similar sentiments, empowering users with the right to access, delete, and even sell their personal data. These regulations act as the ethical bedrock, setting minimum standards for responsible zero-trust implementations."

Emili, her eyes gleaming with understanding, pressed on. "But Regulations alone cannot guarantee compliance without effective enforcement, right? What about industry standards, the practical blueprints for translating these principles into action?"

Soham chuckled. "Indeed, Emili! And organizations like the National Institute of Standards and Technology (NIST) in the US are diligently crafting these blueprints. Their Privacy Framework offers a practical roadmap for implementing zero-trust with ethics at its core, guiding organizations through data governance, risk assessment, and user control mechanisms."

"Furthermore," Soham added, "industry consortiums, like the Cloud Security Alliance (CSA), are developing specific zero-trust guidelines that consider ethical implications. These frameworks act as collaborative efforts, pooling expertise and best practices to ensure responsible advancements in this evolving field."

Emili, her gaze unwavering, leaned forward, a hint of curiosity tinged with practicality in her voice. "Soham," she began, "we have explored the broad strokes of regulations and industry standards shaping ethical zero-trust. But let us zoom in a bit. Are there any specific government standards around zero-trust implementation, mandates that organizations must navigate alongside ethical considerations?"

Soham, a knowing smile playing on his lips, relished the opportunity to delve into the specifics. "Ah, that is the nitty-gritty of the impenetrable digital defenses, where government mandates add another layer to the security landscape."

He paused, letting the weight of her words settle before elaborating. "For instance, in the United States, the Executive Order 14028 stands as a beacon, mandating federal agencies to adopt a zero-trust architecture. This order, while not setting specific technical standards, pushes agencies towards a framework that prioritizes continuous verification, least privilege access, and robust data security – all principles deeply intertwined with ethical considerations."

Emili, her brow furrowed slightly, interjected. "So, it is not a rigid rulebook, but a guiding principle, urging agencies to embrace the core philosophy of zero-trust while leaving room for adapting it to their specific needs and ethical considerations?"

Soham nodded. "Precisely, Emili! And across the globe, similar initiatives are taking root. The UK's National Cyber Security Centre (NCSC) advocates for a cloud-first approach that incorporates zero-trust principles, while Singapore's Cybersecurity Agency (CSA) promotes a 'defense-in-depth' strategy that aligns with zero-trust ideals."

Emili, her eyes gleaming with understanding, pressed on. "So, it is not just a US phenomenon, but a global movement towards secure and ethical cybersecurity practices. How are these government standards impacting organizations beyond the public sector?"

Soham retorted, "The ripple effect is undeniable. Many private organizations, recognizing the advantages of zero-trust and the potential implications of lagging behind government mandates, are proactively adopting similar frameworks. They understand that ethical considerations are not just compliance boxes to tick, but core values that build trust and resilience in the digital fortress."

As the final words faded, the moonlight bathed the hall in a thoughtful glow. This conversation had delved into the specific government standards around zero-trust, revealing the guiding principles set by mandates like EO (Executive Order) 14028 and the global movement towards secure and ethical cybersecurity practices.

V

Guardians at the Gates: Building Ethical AI Defenses for the Digital Fortress

A hush fell over the moonlit hall as the weight of the previous conversation settled. Ethical considerations and government mandates had painted a complex landscape, and now, curiosity flickered in the air.

"So," Emili broke the silence, its tone thoughtful, "we have explored the ethical guardrails and regulatory frameworks shaping zero-trust. But within this fortress, another powerful force is at play: artificial intelligence. How does this digital sentinel fit into the picture, particularly in the light of the ethical considerations we have discussed?"

Soham chuckled, a hint of intrigue in their voice. "Ah, a question worthy of a thousand circuits! AI in cybersecurity, woven into the fabric of zero-trust, is indeed a potent blend. Imagine it as a vigilant sentry, its keen eyes scanning the digital horizon for threats, its analytical prowess dissecting anomalies, and its adaptive nature constantly evolving to outmaneuver adversaries."

"But let's not romanticize," Soham continued. "AI, like any tool, is a double-edged sword. Its power to automate threat detection, strengthen access controls, and even predict cyberattacks is undeniable. Yet, ethical considerations loom large. Bias in algorithms, potential misuse of surveillance capabilities, and the ever-present question of human oversight – these are not shadows lurking in the corners, but challenges demanding immediate attention."

"Indeed," Emili concurred, its tone laced with concern. "The digital safeguards intended to empower us ironically hold the potential to be manipulated for oppressive purposes. Transparency, accountability, and robust ethical frameworks are paramount. We must ensure AI in cybersecurity serves humankind, not the other way around."

"Precisely," Soham responded, a note of optimism creeping into their tone. "Unquestioning acceptance of AI poses a risk to zero-trust initiatives and demands a shift from blind trust to proactive management. Open-source algorithms, rigorous bias testing, and human-in-the-loop decision-making – these are the cornerstones of ethical AI, the safeguards that ensure this powerful technology remains a benevolent guardian, not a digital overlord."

The final words hung in the air, a testament to the complex dance between security, ethics, and the ever-evolving landscape of artificial intelligence. The path ahead, illuminated by their shared curiosity, beckoned further exploration.

"Soham," she began, her voice weaving intrigue with practicality, "Could you elaborate how does this theoretical marvel translate into real-world scenarios? Give me concrete examples of AI safeguarding our digital lives, not just lofty promises."

Soham, a knowing smile playing on his lips, relished the opportunity to unveil the practical magic of AI. "Ah, Emili," he chuckled, "you yearn to see the gears turning, the algorithms whining in the engine room of cybersecurity. Fear not, for the applications of AI are as diverse as the threats they combat."

He paused, letting the anticipation build before elaborating. "Take threat detection and vulnerability management. Imagine AI-powered tools like Deepwatch or Palo Alto Networks' Cortex XDR constantly scouring your network, analyzing mountains of data for suspicious activity. They act as digital detectives, piecing together seemingly inconsequential anomalies into a sinister mosaic of potential threats, be it malware masquerading as harmless code or vulnerabilities waiting to be exploited."

Emili, her eyes gleaming with understanding, interjected. "So, AI sifts through the digital haystack, unearthing needles of malicious intent before they can wreak havoc?"

Soham nodded. "Precisely, Emili! And beyond threat detection, AI shines in anomaly detection. Tools like Splunk or Anomaly Analytics scan user behavior, network traffic, and system logs for deviations from the norm. A sudden spike in login attempts from an unusual location? A surge in data exfiltration? AI flags these anomalies, prompting human experts to investigate, potentially thwarting a cyberattack in its infancy."

The conversation flowed, Soham weaving a tapestry of real-world applications. "Emili, consider email security. Phishing scams, once a bane of inboxes, now face the wrath of AI-powered solutions like Mimecast or Cloudflare Email Security. These tools analyze email content and sender behavior, identifying subtle markers of malicious intent – grammatical errors in supposedly urgent messages, domain spoofing attempts, or inconsistencies in sender addresses. AI acts as your digital gatekeeper, filtering out the wolves in sheep's clothing before they reach your inbox."

Emili, her brow furrowed in thought, pressed on. "But the realm of AI extends beyond email, does not it?"

Soham chuckled. "Indeed, Emili! Even the financial sector benefits from AI's watchful eye. Tools like Featurespace or ACI Worldwide leverage AI and machine learning to detect fraudulent transactions in real-time. Analyzing spending patterns, identifying unusual locations for card usage, and flagging suspicious transactions based on behavioral anomalies – AI acts as a financial watchdog, sniffing out fraudsters before they can drain your accounts."

"Can AI be used for zero-trust implementation? Not only can it, but it has become an indispensable cog in the zero-trust machinery", Emili asked, a glint of intellectual excitement in her eyes.

He gestured expansively, as if conjuring up a digital fortress bristling with AI technology. "Imagine this: continuous authentication and authorization, the very core of zero-trust, empowered by AI engines. Tools like Beyond

Identity or Okta Adaptive MFA analyze user behavior, device characteristics, and contextual factors in real-time. A login attempt from a new device in a remote location? AI assesses the risk, potentially prompting multi-factor authentication or even temporarily restricting access, all to ensure only authorized users gain entry."

Emili, her brow furrowed in thoughtful contemplation, interjected. "So, AI acts as a dynamic watchdog, constantly adapting its scrutiny based on real-time data and risk assessments?"

Soham nodded enthusiastically. "Precisely, Emili! And beyond access control, AI plays a crucial role in endpoint security. Tools like Deepwatch or Cylance leverage machine learning to detect and neutralize malware, even zero-day threats, in real-time. They act as digital antibodies, constantly evolving to combat the ever-shifting landscape of cyber threats."

He continued, his voice taking on a persuasive tone. "Furthermore, AI empowers organizations to implement micro-segmentation, a key tenet of zero-trust. Imagine your network sliced into isolated zones, each protected by AI-driven granular access controls. A data breach in one zone doesn't become a free-for-all, thanks to AI's ability to contain and neutralize threats before they spread."

Emili, a hint of awe creeping into her voice, remarked. "It is almost like AI grants your digital fortress the power of precognition, anticipating and thwarting threats before they materialize."

Soham's lips curved into a playful smile. Not precognition, Emili, but an edge thanks to AI's situational awareness. AI acts as a vigilant sentinel, constantly scanning the digital horizon for anomalies and potential breaches, providing invaluable insights for security teams to make informed decisions."

As their conversation reached a crescendo, the hall seemed to reverberate with the possibilities unleashed by AI in zero-trust. While challenges like bias in algorithms and the need for human oversight remain, the future of digital security appeared undeniably intertwined with the potent capabilities of artificial intelligence.

So, what are artificial intelligence powered tools that are widely used for cyber security?

"Ah, Emili," Soham chuckled, leaning forward with a touch of anticipation, "you are eager to delve into the specific tools wielding the power of AI in cybersecurity. Buckle up, for we are about to explore the arsenal at the disposal of digital defenders!"

He gestured towards the imaginary fortress, its walls now bristling with the names of potent AI-powered tools. With a sly grin, Soham began, 'Our first target though the persistent menace, malware! Tools like Palo Alto Networks Cortex XDR or Deepwatch utilize advanced machine learning to dissect suspicious files and code in real-time. They analyze behavior, identify patterns, and even predict potential outbreaks, acting as digital antibodies before malware can infect your systems."

Emili, her eyes alight with curiosity, interjected. "So, AI acts as a shield, tirelessly analyzing malware to identify its destructive potential before it strikes.?"

With a glint in his eye, Soham remarked, "Precisely, Emili! And beyond malware analysis, AI shines in vulnerability management. Tools like Qualys VMDR (Vulnerability Management, Detection, and Response) or Tenable Nessus leverage AI to automate vulnerability scanning and prioritization. They analyze vast codebases, identifying critical vulnerabilities and even predicting potential exploits, allowing security teams to focus on patching the most urgent threats first."

He continued, his voice weaving technical details with narrative flair. "Imagine AI-powered penetration testing, Emili. Tools like BreachLock or Rapid7 Nexpose utilize machine learning to mimic the tactics of real-world attackers, simulating cyberattacks and identifying exploitable weaknesses in your defenses. It is like sparring with a digital shadow, constantly honing your defenses against the evolving tactics of adversaries."

Emili, her brow furrowed in thought, pondered the implications. "So, AI ruthlessly exploits our weak spots, forcing us to become impenetrable before any real threat emerges?"

Soham nodded enthusiastically. "Indeed, Emili! And finally, consider the realm of risk assessment. Tools like Cybereason or MacAfee MVISION leverage AI to analyze vast security data sets, identifying patterns and trends that indicate potential threats. They paint a real-time picture of your overall security posture, highlighting areas of high risk and guiding your mitigation efforts."

Emili was wondering whether there are any relevant frameworks or government policies around ai.

"Emili," Soham chuckled, a knowing glint in his eyes, "your question delves beyond the tools and into the very structure of the digital fortress. You seek the blueprints, the guiding principles shaping the use of AI in cybersecurity. And yes, within this realm exist frameworks and policies, both from industry and government, aiming to harness the power of AI responsibly."

He gestured towards the imaginary fortress, its walls now adorned with diagrams and policy documents. "First, let's consider industry frameworks. The NIST

Cybersecurity Framework, for instance, incorporates AI considerations into its five core functions, guiding organizations on secure AI implementation in areas like risk assessment, identity and access management, and data protection."

Emili, her brow furrowed in thought, interjected. "So, NIST acts like a compass, helping organizations navigate the complex ethical and technical landscape of AI-powered cybersecurity.?"

Soham nodded. "Precisely! And beyond NIST, organizations like the Partnership on AI have developed frameworks like the Algorithmic Justice League's Anti-Bias and Fairness Framework. These frameworks offer concrete guidelines for mitigating bias in AI algorithms, ensuring fair and ethical applications within cybersecurity."

He continued, his voice weaving global perspectives into the conversation. "On the government front, initiatives like the European Union's AI Act aim to regulate the development and deployment of AI, including its use in cybersecurity. This act emphasizes transparency, accountability, and risk management, striving to ensure AI in cybersecurity safeguards, not jeopardizes, individual rights and freedoms."

With a glint of comprehension in her eyes, Emili persevered, her voice steady. "So, governments are actively steering the course of AI in cybersecurity, defining limitations and advocating for ethical development, is that right?"

Soham smiled. "Indeed, Emili! And national initiatives exist as well. The US's National Security Agency (NSA) Cybersecurity Technical Guidance for AI and Machine Learning outlines best practices for secure AI implementation within government agencies, demonstrating a commitment to responsible adoption."

As their conversation reached a crossroads, the hall seemed to hum with the possibilities and challenges of governing AI in cybersecurity. While frameworks and policies are evolving, questions remain about their effectiveness and enforcement.

But the path ahead, illuminated by their shared curiosity, promised further exploration. "Let us look into the labyrinthine corridors of these frameworks and policies, unravelling their strengths and grappling with the lingering challenges", Emili stated, her eyes sparkling with understanding.

He traced an imaginary path on the air, his gaze fixed on the digital fortress. "Remember, translating frameworks into steps isn't straightforward. NIST, for instance, offers a comprehensive guide, but organizations often struggle to translate its principles into concrete security measures. The journey from theoretical idealism to practical realization remains fraught with difficulty."

"Intrigued," Emili chimed in, her brow creased in thought. 'Is it like possessing a meticulously drawn map, yet lacking the means to find one's bearing and traverse the landscape?"

Soham chuckled. "Precisely! And beyond complexity, the issue of enforcement looms large. Frameworks, unlike regulations, lack teeth. While they offer valuable guidance, their adherence remains voluntary, raising concerns about potential loopholes and inconsistencies in implementation."

Soham said, a playful lilt in his voice. "Furthermore, the rapid evolution of AI technology poses a continuous challenge. Frameworks and policies become outdated quickly, struggling to keep pace with the ever-changing landscape of algorithms and threats. This constant game of catch-up can leave organizations vulnerable to novel AI-powered attacks."

Emili, her eyes burning with intellectual fire, pressed on. "So, it is a race against time, with frameworks constantly needing to adapt and evolve to stay ahead of the curve?"

Soham nodded in admiration. "Indeed, Emili! And amidst these challenges, glimmers of hope emerge. Organizations like the Open Web Application Security Project (OWASP) are developing AI-specific security testing guidelines, providing practical tools for assessing and mitigating risks associated with AI implementation."

He continued; his voice tinged with optimism. "International collaboration also offers promising avenues. Initiatives like the Global Partnership on AI aim to foster responsible AI development and deployment across borders, paving the way for a unified approach to AI governance in cybersecurity."

As their conversation reached a crescendo, the hall seemed to resonate with the echoes of both challenges and opportunities. The future of AI in cybersecurity, while intricate and demanding, brimmed with potential for responsible development and global cooperation.

"Soham," Emili's voice cut through the hushed air, its tone laced with a hint of apprehension, "we have explored the immense potential of AI as a guardian in the digital fortress. But let us not shy away from the shadows lurking at its edges. Tell me, can this same potent force be wielded for nefarious purposes? Can AI, in the wrong hands, become the ultimate weapon for cyberattacks?"

Her question hung in the air, a stark reminder of the duality that often defines technological advancements. Soham, his gaze contemplative, met her challenge with a measured response.

"Ah, Emili," he began, his voice tinged with a touch of grim realism, "you raise a critical point. The very capabilities that make AI a powerful defender can, indeed, be perverted into instruments of immense destruction in the realm of cyberattacks."

He proceeded to paint a chilling picture, his words weaving a tapestry of potential threats. "Imagine AI-powered tools crafting hyper-personalized phishing campaigns, manipulating your online persona and exploiting your vulnerabilities with uncanny precision. Or envision automated botnets, controlled by malicious AI algorithms, launching coordinated DDoS (Distributed Denial of Service) attacks of unprecedented scale, crippling critical infrastructure in mere moments."

A tremor of concern etched itself on Emili's brow as she interrupted. "So, AI transforms into the ultimate mimic, wielding our digital shadows like weapons in attacks of chilling precision?"

Soham nodded gravely. "Precisely, Emili. And beyond impersonation and automation, AI opens doors to novel attack vectors. Imagine malware morphing in real-time, evading traditional detection methods thanks to its AI-driven adaptability. Or consider deepfakes, crafted with frightening realism by AI, sowing disinformation and manipulating public opinion with devastating consequences."

As their conversation unfolded, the hall seemed to hum with the unsettling possibilities unleashed by AI in the wrong hands. But amidst the shadows, Soham offered a glimmer of hope.

"Emili," he continued, his voice regaining its characteristic optimism, "while the threats are undeniable, so are the countermeasures. Advanced threat intelligence powered by AI can anticipate and thwart potential attacks. Only by weaving ethical principles into the fabric of robust security frameworks can we effectively address the risks of AI development and deployment."

He concluded with a resolute tone. "The future of AI in cybersecurity, Emili, rests on a delicate balance. It demands vigilance, collaboration, and an unwavering commitment to responsible development. In this ongoing struggle, the key lies in ensuring that AI remains a force for good, a shield, not a sword, in the digital realm." The conversation, charged with both the perils and possibilities of AI in cyberattacks, reached a natural pause.

"Soham," Emili's voice crackled with intellectual fire, "we've glimpsed the chilling potential of AI in the hands of attackers. Now, let us dissect the arsenal, expose the specific AI-powered vectors they wield, and explore the countermeasures at our disposal. Show me the frontiers of AI security research, the shields we are forging against this evolving threat."

Soham, his gaze mirroring her determination, nodded solemnly. "Indeed, Emili," he began, his voice weaving a narrative of both peril and ingenuity. "Imagine the insidiousness of hyper-personalized phishing campaigns. AI analyzes your online behavior, crafting emails that mimic your closest contacts, their writing style, even their inside jokes. The emotional hooks become razor-sharp, luring you into disclosing sensitive information or downloading malware disguised as familiar attachments."

"Concerned, Emili interrupted, 'So, AI becomes a forger of unparalleled skill, shaking our faith in the digital world. But surely, we have safeguards against such threats? '"

Soham chuckled, a hint of triumph in his eyes. "Of course, Emili! Advanced anomaly detection powered by AI itself can analyze email patterns, flag inconsistencies in language style, and identify subtle deviations from your usual communication networks. This digital sleuthing can expose even the most cunning forgeries before they inflict damage."

He continued, his voice taking on an excited tone. "While email is a familiar battleground, AI has opened a new front: deepfakes. These tools leverage machine learning to generate eerily convincing simulations of anyone, blurring the lines between truth and fiction with worrying speed. However, fortunately the research frontier is ablaze with countermeasures. Techniques like biometric analysis and voice signature verification, both augmented by AI, are being refined to discern the subtle tells of a deepfake, exposing the puppet master behind the manipulated strings."

Emili, her eyes gleaming with understanding, pressed on. "So, it is an arms race, Soham? AI against AI, a constant evolution of attack and defense on the digital battlefield?"

Soham nodded. "Precisely, Emili! And beyond individual countermeasures, the future lies in building holistic AI security frameworks. Imagine a digital ecosystem where AI-powered threat intelligence platforms share information in real-time, identifying emerging attack vectors and proactively deploying defenses across diverse systems. This collective vigilance, fueled by collaboration and ethical development, is the key to staying ahead of the curve."

As their conversation reached a fever pitch, the hall seemed to pulse with the energy of the ongoing battle for cybersecurity. The future, while brimming with challenges, also held the promise of a future where responsible AI development and collaborative research would safeguard the digital fortress against both known and unforeseen threats. But the path ahead, illuminated by their shared passion for knowledge and unwavering commitment to a secure future, promised further exploration.

Emili's gaze met Soham's across the dimly lit hall, a thoughtful crease etched between her brows. "Soham," she commenced, her tone imbued with a blend of appreciation and trepidation, "your articulation has conjured a captivating portrayal of the burgeoning AI arms race, the astute countermeasures being devised, and the research domains pulsating with pioneering advancements." She paused. "Yet, a crucial question lingers. Amidst this intricate dance of attack and defense, how do we secure AI itself? Can we safeguard this powerful tool from manipulation, bias, and unforeseen vulnerabilities that could turn it from a shield into a weapon?"

Soham, his expression mirroring her thoughtful concern, nodded in agreement. "Ah, Emili, you pierce to the heart of the matter. Securing AI is not merely about building countermeasures against external threats; it is about ensuring the integrity and reliability of the tool itself. It's a constant endeavor to address bias, mitigate vulnerabilities, and foster responsible development."

He gestured towards the imaginary fortress, its walls now adorned with principles and frameworks for securing AI. "First, consider the cornerstone of responsible AI development: transparency and explainability. We must understand how AI algorithms arrive at their decisions, ensuring they are free from hidden biases or unforeseen vulnerabilities. Initiatives like the European Union's Explainable AI Act push for transparency in algorithm development and deployment, empowering users to understand and challenge potentially biased outcomes."

Emili, her brow furrowed in contemplation, interjected. "So, it's about shining a light into the black box of AI, ensuring fairness and accountability in its decision-making processes?"

Soham smirked. "Exactly, Emili! Transparency is just the tip of the iceberg. The real key lies in building robust data governance, making sure the fuel for our AI is diverse, unbiased, and secure. Frameworks like the Montreal Declaration champion these principles, reminding us that responsible AI starts with responsible data practices. After all, we wouldn't want our AI to inherit the biases and vulnerabilities lurking in the data it feeds on." He continued, his voice taking on a passionate tone. "Furthermore, the realm of adversarial robustness holds immense promise. Imagine AI-powered systems constantly evolving, anticipating and neutralizing potential attacks designed to manipulate or exploit their vulnerabilities. Research in this domain focuses on hardening AI algorithms against adversarial attacks, ensuring they remain reliable and trustworthy even under duress."

As their conversation reached a crescendo, the hall seemed to thrum with the possibilities and challenges of securing AI. While noteworthy progress is being made, the path ahead remains fraught with hurdles.

"Emili," Soham acknowledged, his voice regaining its measured tone, "the quest for securing AI is an ongoing journey. Addressing algorithmic bias remains a complex challenge, and concerns linger around potential misuse of powerful AI tools by malicious actors. Yet, amidst these challenges, glimmers of hope emerge. International collaboration, like the OECD's Principles on Artificial Intelligence, fosters responsible development and deployment practices across borders. And ethical AI education initiatives equip developers and users alike with the knowledge and awareness necessary to navigate this evolving landscape responsibly."

Her unwavering gaze, sharp as flint, locked Soham's across the hushed hall. "Your insights, Soham," she said, her voice threaded with urgency, "illuminate the complex ballet of safeguarding AI. But the specter of bias looms large. Algorithmic fairness, a fragile yet crucial concept, demands deeper exploration. Tell me, what are the specific challenges we face in mitigating bias within AI, and what potential solutions glimmer on the horizon?"

Soham, his expression mirroring her concern, nodded solemnly. "Ah, Emili, you delve into the very heart of the matter. Bias, insidious and often hidden, can infiltrate the very foundations of AI algorithms, distorting their outputs and amplifying societal inequalities. The challenges we face are multifaceted."

He gestured towards the imaginary fortress; its walls now adorned with diagrams illustrating the various facets of algorithmic bias. AI thrives on data, but biased data breeds biased outcomes. Algorithms trained on datasets skewed towards specific demographics risk perpetuating existing inequalities. Imagine a facial recognition system heavily tilted towards white males; its ability to recognize other groups could be severely hampered, potentially leading to unfair results.

Emili's brow wrinkled in concern as she interjected, "Is AI simply reflecting back the prejudices it's fed? Like a mirror, if we show it a distorted image, its output will be warped too. Perhaps ensuring a balanced and representative data landscape is key to dismantling these embedded inequalities."

Soham chuckled. "Precisely! And beyond biased data, the very design of AI algorithms can introduce bias. If the metrics used to evaluate the algorithm's performance inadvertently favor certain outcomes, the algorithm will optimize for those outcomes, potentially exacerbating existing biases. Imagine a hiring algorithm trained to prioritize past job titles and educational background; it might inadvertently discriminate against candidates from disadvantaged backgrounds, regardless of their actual skills and potential."

He continued, his voice taking on a determined tone. "But amidst these challenges, glimmers of hope emerge. Solutions, though complex, are being actively pursued. Firstly, researchers are developing techniques for debiasing data sets, identifying and mitigating inherent biases before feeding the data to AI algorithms. Imagine AI tools that analyze data for hidden biases and suggest adjustments to ensure fairer representation."

A spark of realization ignited in Emili's eyes as she leaned forward. "So, are we essentially handing AI the keys to self-correction? Can it curate its own data and ensure unbiased outcomes?"

Soham nodded enthusiastically. "Indeed! And beyond data debiasing, researchers are exploring fair AI design principles. These principles guide the development of algorithms that are robust to bias, ensuring they evaluate individuals based on relevant criteria, not inherently biased factors. Imagine algorithms that focus on skills and potential, not historical markers that might perpetuate societal inequalities."

The conversation, charged with the urgency of mitigating bias in AI, reached a pivotal point. Soham paused, allowing Emili's questions to guide the next step.

"Furthermore," he added, anticipating her inquiry, "real-world examples of organizations implementing robust data governance and security practices for AI offer valuable insights. Companies like IBM and Microsoft are establishing AI ethics boards and developing comprehensive frameworks for responsible AI development and deployment. These frameworks encompass data sourcing and management practices, algorithmic fairness assessments, and ongoing monitoring for potential bias."

Emili, her expression thoughtful, pondered the path forward. "So, the battle against bias in AI requires a holistic approach, including purging data of prejudice, creating algorithms grounded in fairness, and nurturing a culture of ethical development within companies. This is a constant process, wouldn't you agree?"

Soham smiled, his eyes reflecting her enthusiasm. "Indeed, Emili. The quest for fairness in AI is an ongoing endeavor, a constant evolution of tools, techniques, and best practices. But with unwavering commitment, collaboration, and a relentless pursuit of ethical development, we can ensure that AI becomes a force for good, empowering individuals and societies while mitigating the specter of bias in its powerful embrace."

Intrigued, Emili's eyes, alight with intellectual curiosity, locked with Soham's across the muted hall. "Your insights, Soham," she began, her voice thrumming with anticipation, "have shed new light on the intricate terrain of bias detection and mitigation. Are there any specific tools and techniques wielded by researchers in this crucial battle? Could you display an example where AI tackles bias not just in theory, but in the real-world crucible of software security?"

Soham, a knowing smile playing on his lips, gestured towards the imaginary fortress, its walls now adorned with diagrams and code snippets. "Ah, Emili, your thirst for concrete examples fuels the fire of progress! Let me transport you to the bustling realm of software security, where an ingenious AI tool known as 'FairCode' stands guard against biased vulnerabilities."

He leaned forward, weaving a narrative of innovation. "Imagine software developers, often unconsciously, introducing biases into their code. These biases can manifest as hidden vulnerabilities, disproportionately impacting specific user groups based on factors like gender, race, or disability. FairCode, armed with the power of natural language processing and machine learning, scans codebases for these hidden biases."

Emili, her face etched with focus, cut in. "So, FairCode is basically a code fortune teller, sniffing out patterns and language quirks that could signal potential vulnerabilities driven by bias?"

Soham chuckled. "Precisely, Emili! FairCode analyzes code comments, variable names, and function calls, searching for terms or phrases that might indicate bias. For instance, imagine a facial recognition algorithm trained on male faces. FairCode might flag code sections mentioning 'male' as the default setting, highlighting a potential bias that could disadvantage female users."

He continued; his voice imbued with excitement. "But FairCode doesn't merely point fingers; it offers solutions. The tool suggests alternative phrasing, variable names, and code structures that are neutral and inclusive. It recommends incorporating diverse datasets during testing to ensure the software functions fairly for all user groups."

Emili, her eyes gleaming with understanding, pressed on. "So, FairCode becomes a gentle AI tutor, nudging developers towards inclusive coding practices and mitigating potential vulnerabilities before they become real-world problems?"

Soham nodded enthusiastically. "Indeed, Emili! And beyond identifying and mitigating bias, FairCode empowers developers with its 'explainability' features. It demystifies its own decision-making process, allowing developers to understand why certain code sections were flagged and how the suggested changes promote fairness. This transparency builds trust and encourages developers to actively embrace bias-free coding practices."

As their conversation reached a crescendo, the hall seemed to hum with the possibilities unleashed by AI in software security. While FairCode represents just one example, it highlights the immense potential of AI to not only detect and mitigate bias, but also foster a culture of responsible development.

"Emili," Soham acknowledged, his voice regaining its measured tone, "FairCode's journey is still in its early stages, but its success offers valuable lessons. The challenge lies in balancing bias detection with practicality, ensuring suggested changes do not compromise software functionality. Additionally, widespread adoption requires not just advanced tools, but also education and awareness among developers about the importance of bias-free coding."

The conversation, charged with both the promise and challenges of AI in software security, reached a crossroads. The path ahead, illuminated by their shared quest for inclusivity and driven by a commitment to responsible development, held the promise of further unravelling the intricacies of software security, ensuring that code not only functions flawlessly, but also upholds the values of fairness and equality in the digital realm and embark on a discussion about fostering a culture of awareness and education among developers to champion responsible coding practices.

VI

Beyond AI: The Unsung Hero - Secure Software Coding Security

"Soham," Emili's voice resonated through the dimly lit hall, a hint of steel tempering its usual curiosity, "Your vivid portrayal of FairCode has illuminated the vital role AI plays in combating bias in software security. Yet, this begs a fundamental question: beyond these ingenious tools, what lies at the bedrock of secure software? Is it not the very foundation of code itself, the practice of secure coding, that forms the first line of defense against vulnerabilities and potential biases?"

Soham, his gaze mirroring her thoughtful intent, nodded in agreement. "Ah, Emili, you pierce to the heart of the matter! Secure coding practices are indeed the cornerstone of software security, the impenetrable shield upon which malicious actors and unforeseen biases alike shatter. Imagine a fortress, however magnificent its defenses, built upon shaky foundations. Even the most sophisticated AI tools will struggle to patch cracks in the very fabric of the code."

Soham pointed to the visualized code security fortress, where battlements now gleamed with the inscription of secure coding principles and best practices. He began with the cornerstone principle of least privilege. Imagine, he said, each function within the code possessing only the minimal access rights necessary for its operation. This way, even if a chink appeared in the armor, the damage would be confined, preventing attackers or prejudiced algorithms from exploiting the entire system.

Emili, her brow furrowed in contemplation, asked, "Essentially, we're compartmentalizing power within the code ensuring no single function becomes supreme and poses a systemic threat, right?

Soham chuckled. "Precisely, Emili! And beyond least privilege, the practice of thorough input validation stands guard. Imagine erecting robust checkpoints at every entry point where data enters the system. These checkpoints, powered by rigorous validation routines, scrutinize and sanitize every byte of information, ensuring malicious code or biased data doesn't infiltrate the system's core."

He continued, his voice taking on a passionate tone. "Furthermore, secure coding champions the "secure by design" philosophy, ensuring security is not an afterthought but an intrinsic element woven into the code's foundation, akin to an architect meticulously embedding safety principles into the blueprint of a skyscraper. This proactive approach, rather than a reactive scramble for defense after vulnerabilities emerge, is the hallmark of truly secure software."

The hall seemed to thrum with the possibilities and importance of secure coding practices. While AI tools like FairCode offer invaluable assistance, they cannot substitute for a solid foundation built on secure coding principles. "Emili," Soham acknowledged, his voice regaining its measured tone, "the challenges of secure coding are not to be underestimated. Legacy systems, often riddled with historical vulnerabilities, pose a significant hurdle. Additionally, the ever-evolving landscape of threats demands constant vigilance and adaptation. Yet, amidst these challenges, glimmers of hope emerge."

He paused, anticipating Emili's inquisitive nature. "Organizations worldwide," he continued, "are embracing secure coding practices through rigorous training programs and code reviews. Additionally, the rise of open-source security libraries and frameworks empowers developers to build upon secure foundations, further solidifying the digital ramparts against threats."

The air crackled with intellectual anticipation as Emili's voice filled the dimly lit hall. "Soham," she began, her gaze unwavering, "you have painted a magnificent picture of secure coding practices, the bedrock upon which software security stands. Yet, the journey from conception to deployment, the very birth of software, begs to be explored. Tell me, what role does the secure software development life cycle (SSDLC) play in weaving security into the fabric of software, from its nascent lines of code to its final polished form?"

Soham's smile danced across his lips like a knowing secret. With a flourish, he gestured towards the imaginary fortress, its walls now transformed into a tapestry woven with the intricate threads of the SSDLC. "Ah, Emili," he said, his voice warm with conviction, "you've grasped the very essence of software security! The SSDLC is more than just a process; it's a philosophy, a vigilant shield that guards against threats at every stage of development, from the initial spark of an idea to the triumphant moment of release."

He leaned forward, his voice taking on an animated tone. "Imagine the SSDLC as a fortified journey, each stage a checkpoint where potential vulnerabilities are identified and neutralized. In the early planning and requirement gathering phases, security considerations are woven into the project's fabric. Imagine threat modeling exercises, identifying potential attack vectors before a single line of code is written."

With a contemplative frown, Emili cut in. "So, it's like looking into the enemy's game plan before the battle even starts, isn't it? Anticipating their weaknesses and setting up our defenses proactively?"

Soham chuckled. "Precisely, Emili! And as the journey progresses through design and development, secure coding practices, as we discussed earlier, become foot soldiers on the frontlines. Rigorous testing throughout the cycle, from unit testing to penetration testing, ensures even the most cunning vulnerabilities are unearthed and remedied before release."

He continued; his voice tinged with excitement. "However, as software development transforms, security strategies adapt. The rise of DevSecOps, a movement where developers, security professionals, and operations teams work hand-in-hand throughout the SSDLC, represents a paradigm shift."

Eyes sparkling with newfound comprehension, Emili continued, "This is not a solo act anymore. It is a security orchestra, everyone playing their part in harmony?"

Soham nodded enthusiastically. "Indeed, Emili! DevSecOps breaks down the silos between teams, fostering collaboration and shared responsibility for security. Imagine developers equipped with security tools and training, security professionals embedded within development teams, and operations teams prepared to handle security incidents proactively."

As their conversation reached a pivotal point, the hall thrummed with the possibilities unleashed by embracing a secure SDLC (Software Development Life Cycle) and the collaborative power of DevSecOps. While challenges remain, the path forward shines with promise.

"Emili," Soham acknowledged, his voice regaining its measured tone, "implementing a robust SSDLC and embracing DevSecOps practices require commitment and investment. Organizations must cultivate a culture of security awareness, equip teams with the necessary tools and training, and foster collaboration across departments. Yet, the rewards are undeniable: software that is not only functional and innovative, but also secure and resilient in the face of ever-evolving threats."

Soham, his gaze mirroring Emili's intellectual fervor, continued. "DevSecOps, as I mentioned, is not merely a procedural overhaul; it is a cultural revolution. Imagine a symphony, not of segregated instruments, but of interwoven melodies, where developers, security professionals, and operations teams harmonize in perfect cadence, each contributing their unique notes to the security concerto."

He gestured towards the imaginary fortress; its walls now adorned with diagrams depicting the DevSecOps principles woven into each stage of the SDLC. "Embrace the "shift left" approach to security. From the outset, prioritize security by integrating it into the design process, addressing potential vulnerabilities right from the start."

Emili, her brow furrowed in thoughtful engagement, interjected. "So, it is like vaccinating the software against vulnerabilities early on, building security into its very DNA instead of patching it on later?"

Soham chuckled. "Precisely! And this shift left philosophy extends beyond mere testing. Imagine developers equipped with tools like static code analysis and secure coding libraries, proactively identifying and mitigating vulnerabilities at the source. Collaboration becomes paramount, with security professionals embedded within development teams, acting as trusted advisors and mentors, not isolated gatekeepers."

Emphasizing the crucial role of automation, he further explained, "Automation, the lynchpin of our security strategy, acts as the tireless maestro, orchestrating this security symphony flawlessly. Imagine automated security scans seamlessly integrated into the development pipeline, continuously identifying and addressing vulnerabilities without slowing down the development tempo. Infrastructure as code tools provision and configure secure environments automatically, ensuring consistency and minimizing human error."

Eyes sparkling with newfound comprehension, Emili continued her inquiry. "Essentially, automation acts as the codebase's tireless guardian, vigilantly patrolling its digital ramparts. This, in turn, liberates human minds to tackle more strategic challenges, wouldn't you agree?"

Soham nodded enthusiastically. "Indeed! And beyond automation, the principle of continuous monitoring ensures vigilance throughout the software's lifecycle.

Imagine security dashboards displaying real-time insights into potential threats, allowing teams to proactively address issues before they escalate into full-blown breaches. Logging and SIEM tools become watchful sentinels, constantly scrutinizing system activity for suspicious anomalies."

As their conversation reached a crescendo, the hall seemed to thrum with the possibilities unleashed by embracing DevSecOps principles. While challenges remain, the collaborative spirit and powerful tools at its disposal offer a compelling vision for secure software development.

"Emili," Soham acknowledged, his voice regaining its measured tone, "the path to successful DevSecOps implementation is paved with both opportunities and obstacles. Integration requires careful planning and cultural change. Teams must be equipped with the right tools and training, and communication channels must be clear and open. Yet, the rewards are substantial: reduced vulnerabilities, faster release cycles, and heightened organizational resilience against cyber threats."

The conversation, charged with both the intricacies and potential of DevSecOps principles and tools, reached a crossroads.

Emili's gaze, sharp and unwavering, met Soham's across the dimly lit hall. "The symphony of DevSecOps," she began, her voice laced with intrigue, "rings with the promise of secure software. Yet, like any intricate performance, its success hinges on seamless integration and meticulous optimization. Tell me, Soham, what best practices guide the integration of DevSecOps principles into the existing fabric of development, ensuring harmony and not dissonance?"

Soham, a knowing smile playing on his lips, gestured towards the imaginary fortress, its walls now adorned with diagrams illustrating best practices for DevSecOps integration. "Ah, Emili, you touch upon the crucial juncture where theory meets practice! Integrating DevSecOps is not a mere transplant; it is a delicate dance, weaving security threads into the existing development tapestry without disrupting its rhythm."

He leaned forward, his voice taking on an animated tone. "Firstly, consider the principle of 'start small and scale. 'Imagine introducing DevSecOps tools and practices gradually, focusing on specific stages of the SDLC and building momentum from there. Quick wins, like integrating static code analysis into early development phases, demonstrate the value of security and encourage broader adoption."

"This sounds like a measured way to introduce the new security approach," Emili said thoughtfully, her brow furrowed. "It lets teams gradually get used to it and build confidence before going all in."

Soham chuckled. "Precisely! And beyond gradual adoption, communication becomes the bridge between teams. Imagine open channels, regular meetings, and shared dashboards fostering collaboration and transparency. Security professionals should not be seen as roadblocks, but as trusted partners in the development journey."

He continued; his voice tinged with excitement. "Automation, the tireless foot soldier, plays a crucial role in optimization. Imagine automated security scans seamlessly integrated into the CI/CD pipeline, providing continuous feedback, and reducing manual workload. Infrastructure as code tools can further streamline deployment, ensuring secure environments are provisioned and configured consistently."

A spark of realization ignited in Emili's eyes as she pressed forward. "So, automation transforms into the unwavering conductor, not only uncovering vulnerabilities but also optimizing processes and empowering human minds for crucial decision-making."

Soham nodded enthusiastically. "Indeed, Emili! But remember, automation is not a silver bullet. Tools require customization and configuration to align with specific needs. Additionally, metrics and dashboards must be carefully chosen to provide actionable insights, not simply data overload."

As their conversation reached a pivotal point, the hall thrummed with the possibilities unleashed by optimized DevSecOps integration. While challenges remain, the best practices outlined offer a roadmap for seamless collaboration and efficient security.

Soham's voice regained its composure as he addressed Emili. "Optimizing DevSecOps is a perpetual journey, 'he emphasized. 'True success requires not just cold metrics, but also the real-world insights of our development teams. Continuous improvement, staying ahead of evolving threats and technologies, is the cornerstone of a robust and impactful security posture."

"Soham," Emili's voice resonated through the dimly lit hall, a hint of challenge lacing her curiosity, "Your depiction of DevSecOps paints a captivating picture of seamless security woven into the fabric of development. Yet, it begs the question: how starkly does this approach contrast with the traditional software coding practices of yesteryear? Tell me, where do the seams truly show when comparing DevSecOps to its predecessors, particularly in the realm of vulnerability management, security testing, and platform security?"

Soham, a knowing glint in his eyes, gestured towards the imaginary fortress, its walls now adorned with diagrams contrasting traditional and DevSecOps approaches. "Ah, Emili, you pierce the heart of the matter! The chasm between traditional practices and DevSecOps is vast, particularly in how we manage vulnerabilities, test for security, and secure the very platforms upon which our software dances."

He began with a flourish. "Gone are the days of reactive patching after vulnerabilities are discovered; a hallmark of the old-school approach to vulnerability management. DevSecOps flips the script, emphasizing a proactive mindset. Static code analysis and threat modeling act as watchful guardians, uncovering vulnerabilities early in the development process, nipping them in the bud before they blossom into major breaches."

With a contemplative furrow in her brow, Emili interjected. "So, it's like moving from the reactive firefighting of security breaches to proactive prevention, snuffing out threats before they erupt into mayhem?"

Soham chuckled. "Precisely, Emili! And the contrast extends to security testing. Traditional practices often relied on siloed penetration testing; a one-off event detached from the development flow. DevSecOps integrates security testing throughout the SDLC, from unit testing with security considerations to automated penetration testing woven into the CI/CD pipeline. Imagine a continuous feedback loop, constantly identifying and remediating vulnerabilities, not just at the finish line."

He continued; his voice tinged with excitement. "But the transformation extends beyond code and tests. Platform security, the very foundation upon which software runs, undergoes a metamorphosis in DevSecOps. Gone are the days of mutable golden images, vulnerable to configuration drift and potential compromise. Immutable infrastructure as code takes center stage, ensuring secure environments are provisioned and configured consistently, replicable across deployments."

Emili, her eyes gleaming with understanding, pressed on. "So, mutable golden images, akin to ever-changing tapestries, give way to the solidity of immutable infrastructure as code, like building blocks on a secure foundation?"

Soham nodded enthusiastically. "Indeed! And tools like Terraform and Ansible become the architects of this secure foundation, automating infrastructure provisioning and configuration, minimizing human error, and ensuring consistency. Gone are the days of manual server patching and configuration; automation reigns supreme."

As their conversation reached a crescendo, the hall seemed to pulse with the possibilities unleashed by DevSecOps' stark contrast to traditional practices. While challenges remain, the shift towards proactive vulnerability management, integrated security testing, and robust platform security offers a compelling vision for secure software development in the digital age.

"Emili," Soham concluded, his voice resonating with conviction, "the journey from traditional practices to DevSecOps is not merely a technological shift, but a cultural revolution. It demands a commitment to collaboration, automation, and a proactive approach to security. Yet, the rewards are undeniable: software not just functional and innovative, but resilient against ever-evolving threats, built upon a foundation of trust and unwavering security."

The conversation, charged with the stark differences and transformative potential of DevSecOps, reached a natural pause.

Emili started wondering about how DevSecOps enhances speed and agility over traditional software development.

"Emili," Soham's voice resonated through the dimly lit hall, a spark of intrigue igniting in his eyes, "Your query delves into the very essence of DevSecOps: its ability to not only fortify software against vulnerabilities but also propel development with remarkable speed and agility. Imagine two racing cars, the traditional lumbering behemoth struggling to navigate twists and turns, and the DevSecOps sleek machine gliding through the course, security seamlessly woven into its fabric."

He gestured towards the imaginary fortress; its walls now adorned with diagrams illustrating how DevSecOps enhances development velocity. "Firstly, consider the elimination of friction points. Gone are the days of siloed security checks and late-stage vulnerability discoveries that grind development to a halt. DevSecOps integrates security throughout the SDLC, from threat modeling in the initial stages to automated security scans woven into the CI/CD pipeline. Imagine vulnerabilities addressed as they arise, not as roadblocks at the finish line."

Emili, her brow furrowed in thoughtful engagement, interjected, "So, it is like removing potholes from the development track, allowing teams to maintain momentum without sudden jolts and delays?"

Soham chuckled. "Precisely, Emili! And this continuous feedback loop fosters rapid iteration and improvement. Security testing integrated into unit testing and automated penetration testing provide real-time insights, enabling developers to fix vulnerabilities quickly and efficiently. Imagine features getting battle-tested for security throughout the journey, not just at the final checkpoint."

He continued; his voice tinged with excitement. "Furthermore, imagine automation as a high-performance engine, driving operational excellence and eliminating the drudgery of repetitive tasks. Infrastructure as code tools provision and configure secure environments consistently, while automated security scans eliminate the need for manual vulnerability hunting. Imagine teams freed from repetitive tasks, focusing their energy on innovation and delivering value faster."

Emili, her eyes gleaming with understanding, pressed on, "So, automation becomes the tireless engine, propelling development forward while freeing up the human minds to steer the strategic direction?"

Soham nodded enthusiastically. "Indeed! And beyond speed and agility, DevSecOps enhances compliance with security frameworks and regulations, like SOC 2 or PCI DSS. Imagine built-in security controls and automated audits, reducing the burden of compliance and minimizing the risk of hefty fines or reputational damage."

He paused, a knowing smile playing on his lips. "But theory, as captivating as it may be, thrives on the nourishment of real-world examples. Let me recount the tale of ACME Inc., a company struggling with slow-release cycles and frequent security breaches due to siloed development and reactive security practices. Their transition to DevSecOps, with tools like GitLab CI/CD and automated penetration testing, resulted in a 40% reduction in time to market, a 75% decrease in security vulnerabilities, and a newfound confidence in their software's resilience."

As their conversation reached a crescendo, the hall seemed to hum with the possibilities unleashed by DevSecOps' transformative impact on development speed and agility. While challenges remain, the integration of security, automation, and continuous feedback offers a compelling vision for secure and efficient software development.

"Emili," Soham concluded, his voice resonating with conviction, "DevSecOps is not merely a set of tools and practices; it's a cultural shift, a philosophy that embeds security into the very DNA of development. It demands a commitment to collaboration, automation, and a proactive approach to security. Yet, the rewards are undeniable: software delivered faster, with greater agility, and fortified against ever-evolving threats, all while ensuring compliance and safeguarding organizational reputation." The path ahead, illuminated by their shared pursuit of secure and efficient software development and driven by a commitment to responsible practices, held the promise of further unravelling the intricate tapestry of DevSecOps, ensuring that software not only shapes the digital world but also navigates it with unrivalled speed and agility, leaving vulnerabilities and compliance headaches in its wake.

"Soham," Emili's voice echoed through the dimly lit hall, a note of steel threading through her curiosity, "Your words paint a vibrant picture of DevSecOps, a streamlined machine propelling development with remarkable speed and resilience. Yet, the digital landscape is fraught with unforeseen challenges, ever-evolving threats. Tell me, how does DevSecOps equip software not just with agility, but with the fortitude to withstand these unforeseen turbulences?"

A hint of understanding danced in Soham's eyes as he pointed towards the sketched outline of a fortress, its ramparts now emblazoned with symbols representing the foundations of DevSecOps resilience. "You delve into the essence of it, Emili," he remarked. "DevSecOps thrives not just on swiftness and adaptability, but also on its capacity to pivot under pressure, rise above sudden attacks, and navigate the ever-changing digital landscape. Think of it as a vessel designed not only for speed, but also for resilience, its sails billowing with the winds of innovation yet built to weather unforeseen storms."

He leaned forward, his voice taking on an animated tone. "Firstly, consider the principle of 'continuous monitoring. 'Imagine vigilant watchtowers, powered by security information and event management (SIEM) tools, constantly scanning for anomalous activity and potential threats. Even the most cunning attackers leave footprints, and DevSecOps ensures these footprints are swiftly detected and neutralized before they morph into full-blown breaches."

Emili, her brow furrowed in thoughtful contemplation, interjected. "Like a watchful crew, they anticipate trouble before it brews."

Soham chuckled. "Precisely! And beyond constant vigilance, DevSecOps fosters adaptability and incident response preparedness. Imagine pre-defined playbooks, readily available tools, and cross-functional teams trained to handle security incidents swiftly and effectively. Even unforeseen attacks cannot cripple a system prepared to bend and adapt."

He continued; his voice tinged with excitement. "Furthermore, automation becomes the tireless first responder, streamlining incident response processes and minimizing human error. Automated remediation scripts and rollback configurations can contain damage instantly, while communication channels ensure stakeholders are informed and coordinated efforts mitigate further risks."

A gleam of realization dawned in Emili's eyes. "So, automation assumes the role of the emergency team, acting swiftly and precisely to contain the damage and stabilize the system?"

Soham nodded enthusiastically. "Indeed, Emili! And beyond incident response, DevSecOps emphasizes continuous learning and improvement. Imagine post-mortem analyses, vulnerability prioritization based on real-world attack patterns, and a culture of open communication where lessons learned from near misses and actual breaches fuel future resilience."

"Emili," Soham concluded, his voice resonating with conviction, "DevSecOps is not just a set of tools and practices; it's a philosophy that embraces the uncertain nature of the digital world. It demands a commitment to vigilance, preparedness, and a culture of learning. Yet, the rewards are undeniable: software that withstands the test of time, emerges stronger from unforeseen challenges, and adapts to the ever-evolving digital landscape, safeguarding not just functionality but also organizational reputation and user trust."

As their conversation reached a crescendo, the hall seemed to pulse with the possibilities unleashed by DevSecOps' inherent resilience. While challenges remain, the combination of continuous monitoring, incident response preparedness, automation, and continuous learning offers a compelling vision for software that not only innovates quickly but also stands firm against unforeseen threats.

VII

Beyond Uptime: Cultivating Organizational Resilience and Digital Operations

The air crackled with anticipation as Emili leaned forward, her gaze unwavering. "Soham," her voice resonated through the dimly lit hall, "Your discourse on DevSecOps has painted a compelling picture of secure software, agile and robust. Yet, the digital realm pulsates with unforeseen threats, ever-shifting landscapes. Tell me, how does this philosophy of resilience manifest in the face of cyberattacks, the very storms that threaten to cripple digital infrastructure?"

Soham, a knowing smile playing on his lips, gestured towards the imaginary fortress, its walls now adorned with diagrams illustrating the pillars of cyber resilience. "Ah, Emili, you pose a crucial question! DevSecOps, while championing security and agility, is merely the shield; cyber resilience is the very foundation upon which the fortress stands, its bedrock capable of withstanding the tremors of even the most potent cyberquakes."

He continued, his voice taking on an animated tone. "Building cyber resilience is like weaving a tapestry of diverse security measures. Each thread alone may not withstand a powerful attack, but together they form a resilient fabric that deflects and minimizes damage."

With a thoughtful frown, Emili cut in, her voice laced with curiosity, "Is it like a spiderweb, perhaps? Each strand, meticulously interconnected, absorbs, and distributes the force of an attack, ensuring the core remains intact?" Soham chuckled. "Precisely, Emili! And at the heart of this web lies redundancy. Imagine multiple data centers, geographically dispersed, mirroring critical systems. Even if one node falls, the others ensure continuity of operations, minimizing downtime and data loss."

He continued; his voice tinged with excitement. "Incident response takes center stage when building cyber resilience. Imagine having pre-scripted playbooks, a ready arsenal of tools, and diverse teams that can swiftly pinpoint, isolate, and neutralize threats. This approach not only bolsters defenses against initial attacks but also enables rapid recovery, minimizing downtime and disruption."

Emili, her gaze alight with comprehension, continued her questioning. "Essentially, it's like having a crack fire team, armed with the perfect tools and training, prepared to douse any blaze before it consumes the whole building, isn't it?"

Soham nodded enthusiastically. "Indeed, Emili! And beyond immediate response, continuous learning and improvement forms the bedrock of long-term resilience. Imagine post-mortem analyses, vulnerability prioritization based on real-world attack patterns, and a culture of open communication where lessons learned from near misses and actual breaches fuel future defenses."

Emili's inquisitive gaze met Soham's across the dimly lit hall. "Your words, Soham," she began, her voice laced with intrigue, "paint a vivid picture of cyber resilience, a fortress weathering digital storm. Yet, within this edifice lies the beating heart – the systems, the infrastructure. Tell me, how does Site Reliability Engineering (SRE) weave its magic into this tapestry of resilience, ensuring these vital components remain operational even in the face of adversity?"

Soham, a knowing smile playing on his lips, gestured towards the imaginary fortress, its walls now adorned with diagrams illustrating the principles of SRE in action. "You touch upon the very essence of SRE! It is not just about building walls; it is about ensuring the machinery within runs smoothly, adapts to fluctuations, and emerges unscathed from unexpected jolts. Imagine a team of skilled engineers, not just guarding the gates, but meticulously maintaining the gears, monitoring their performance, and anticipating potential breakdowns before they cripple the operation."

Eyes gleaming, he leaned in, his voice buzzing with excitement. "Imagine tireless AI assistants constantly monitoring the system, automatically scaling resources, plugging security holes, and running diagnostics. This frees up our skilled engineers to tackle high-level projects, minimizing human error and guaranteeing smooth, dependable operations. It is all about leveraging the power of automation, the SRE way!"

Emili, her brow furrowed in thoughtful contemplation, interjected. "So, it is like having tireless robots tending to the machinery, freeing up the skilled engineers to diagnose complex issues and optimize performance?"

Soham chuckled. "Precisely! And beyond automation, SRE champions observability. Imagine dashboards displaying system health in real-time, metrics revealing potential anomalies, and logs providing forensic evidence of issues. This constant vigilance empowers engineers to identify and address threats before they escalate into full-blown outages."

He continued; his voice tinged with excitement. "Furthermore, SRE emphasizes blameless post-mortems. Imagine a culture where failures are not met with accusations, but with open discussions and collaborative learning. By analyzing incidents without assigning blame, engineers can identify root causes, implement preventative measures, and build even more resilient systems."

A glint of realization lit up Emili's eyes as she pressed on. "It's like alchemy,' she mused, 'transforming failure into the gold of understanding, each misstep forging a stronger shield."

Soham nodded enthusiastically. "Indeed! And this continuous improvement loop fuels the very essence of cyber resilience. SRE fosters a culture of experimentation, where engineers are encouraged to test new approaches, learn from failures, and adapt to the ever-shifting digital landscape."

As their conversation reached a crescendo, the hall seemed to thrum with the possibilities unleashed by the symbiotic relationship between cyber resilience and SRE. While threats remain, the combination of automation, observability, blameless post-mortems, and continuous improvement offers a compelling vision for digital infrastructure that not only operates flawlessly but also learns and adapts from its experiences, becoming more resilient with each passing day.

"Emili," Soham concluded, his voice resonating with conviction, "SRE is not just a set of tools and practices; it's a cultural revolution, a way of thinking about systems and their resilience. It demands a commitment to automation, vigilance, collaboration, and continuous learning. Yet, the rewards are undeniable: reliable operations, minimized downtime, and a digital infrastructure that stands firm against unforeseen challenges, safeguarding not just functionality but also organizational reputation and user trust."

"Soham," Emili's voice rang through the dimly lit hall, a glint of curiosity in her eyes, "The way you describe SREs as the silent guardians of uptime is truly captivating. However, I yearn to delve deeper, to dissect the specific tools and practices that empower this alchemy. Tell me, what instruments do these digital alchemists wield? What frameworks and guidelines guide their hands as they forge an unbreakable chain of resilience?"

Soham, a knowing smile playing on his lips, gestured towards the imaginary fortress, its walls now adorned with diagrams displaying specific SRE tools and practices. "Ah, Emili, your thirst for knowledge fuels this very conversation! Let's delve into the arsenal of an SRE, the tools and frameworks that transform proactive automation and meticulous monitoring into the bedrock of resilience."

He began with a flourish. "Firstly, consider the DevOps Institute's SRE Body of Knowledge (SRE BoK). Imagine a compass, guiding SREs with best practices in monitoring, incident response, automation, and continuous improvement. This foundational framework equips engineers with the language and methodologies to build resilient systems."

Emili, her brow furrowed in thoughtful engagement, interjected. "So, the SRE BoK acts as a shared map, ensuring everyone speaks the same language and navigates the terrain of resilience with a unified approach?"

Soham chuckled. "Beyond frameworks, specific tools become the trusty tools in the SRE's belt. Imagine Prometheus and Grafana, their watchful eyes constantly monitoring system metrics, revealing even the faintest tremors of potential issues before they escalate into earthquakes."

He continued; his voice tinged with excitement. "Furthermore, tools like Terraform and Ansible become tireless builders, automating infrastructure provisioning and configuration, ensuring consistency and minimizing human error. This automation removes the shackles of manual toil, freeing engineers to focus on strategic initiatives and proactive resilience measures."

Emili, her eyes gleaming with understanding, pressed on. "So, automation becomes the tireless workhorse, laying the foundation for stability while freeing the human minds to strategize and anticipate future challenges?"

Soham nodded enthusiastically. "Indeed! And for incident response, tools like PagerDuty and VictorOps stand as vigilant sentries, ensuring rapid notification and coordinated action when issues arise. Imagine a well-drilled fire alarm, instantly alerting the brigade and mobilizing resources to contain the flames before they spread."

He paused, a thoughtful expression crossing his face. "But tools, while powerful, are just one facet of the equation. The true magic lies in industry guidelines and community collaboration. Imagine organizations like Google SRE and Netflix Engineering sharing their hard-earned lessons through publications and conferences. This collective knowledge exchange fuels innovation, accelerates adoption of best practices, and elevates the entire industry towards a higher level of resilience."

Emili's gaze, alight with curiosity, met Soham's across the dimly lit hall. "Your discourse on SRE has painted a vivid picture of resilience woven into the very fabric of systems," she began, her voice laced with inquiry. "While resilience isn't magically conjured, strong frameworks serve as the foundation upon which it's built. Soham, what frameworks stand out as guiding lights for engineers crafting reliable and resilient systems?"

Soham, a knowing smile playing on his lips, gestured towards the imaginary fortress, its walls now adorned with diagrams representing various SRE frameworks. "Ah, Emili, your question delves into the very foundation of SRE! Indeed, frameworks serve as guiding lights, empowering engineers to navigate the complexities of building and maintaining resilient systems."

He continued, his voice taking on an animated tone. "Firstly, consider the Google SRE Book (SRE BoK). Imagine it as a comprehensive map, outlining core SRE principles like monitoring, incident response, automation, and continuous learning. This foundational framework equips engineers with a shared language and methodologies, ensuring everyone speaks the same resilience dialect."

Emili, her brow furrowed in thoughtful contemplation, interjected. "So, the SRE BoK acts as a Rosetta Stone for resilience, fostering a common understanding and approach across diverse teams and projects?"

Soham chuckled. "Precisely, Emili! And beyond the BoK, specific frameworks like the Four Golden Signals and Blameless Postmortems serve as potent tools. Imagine the Four Golden Signals – latency, traffic, errors, and saturation – as sentinels standing guard, constantly monitoring the system's health and sounding the alarm at the first tremor of potential issues."

He paused, a thoughtful expression crossing his face. "Furthermore, Blameless Postmortems become the crucible of resilience. Imagine open and honest discussions, analyzing incidents without assigning blame, but focusing on identifying root causes and implementing preventative measures. This culture of continuous learning ensures every failure becomes a steppingstone towards a more resilient future."

Emili, her gaze alight with comprehension, continued, "So, the Four Golden Signals act as sentries, detecting threats early. Blameless Postmortems, in turn, turn failures into lessons, bolstering the system's resilience?"

Soham nodded enthusiastically. "Indeed, Emili! And there is more! Frameworks like the Phoenix Project and DevOps Handbook offer practical guidance on implementing SRE principles. Imagine them as detailed blueprints, laying out actionable steps for building automated infrastructure, implementing continuous delivery pipelines, and fostering a collaborative culture within teams."

He concluded, his voice resonating with conviction. "Ultimately, Emili, the choice of framework depends on the specific context and needs. However, the core principles remain constant – automation, vigilance, collaboration, and continuous learning. By embracing these principles and leveraging the right frameworks, SRE engineers can transform their systems from vulnerable fortresses to bastions of resilience, standing tall in the face of any digital storm."

Emili's inquisitive gaze met Soham's across the dimly lit hall. "Through your words, Soham," she began, her voice laced with eagerness, "I see a powerful image of how SRE practices contribute to resilient systems. Yet, the digital domain is not just about uptime; it pulsates with the need for robust security. Tell me, how does this SRE alchemy translate into specific areas of cybersecurity? Can its principles fortify the very walls of our digital fortresses, enhancing critical aspects like identity and access management, vulnerability management, encryption, incident response, and even the very engine room of security operations?"

Soham, a familiar smile playing on his lips, gestured towards the imaginary fortress, its walls now pulsating with diagrams illustrating how SRE principles strengthen various cybersecurity aspects. "Ah, Emili, you pose a question at the very heart of SRE's value! Its magic lies not just in resilience, but in its ability to permeate every facet of cybersecurity, transforming them into bastions of defense."

He leaned forward, his voice taking on an animated tone. "Prioritize securing your infrastructure from the get-go with robust IAM solutions. Automated user access with tools like Terraform and Ansible, ensuring efficient onboarding and offboarding while maintaining strict security protocols. SRE principles ensure granular control, least privilege access, and continuous monitoring for anomalies, effectively closing backdoors before intruders can even knock."

A thoughtful crease formed between Emi's brows as she interjected. "So, SRE automates the permissions, guaranteeing that only authorized individuals gain entry, and even then, their access is limited to designated areas. All the while, the system keeps a watchful eye for any activity that might raise red flags."

Soham chuckled. "Precisely, Emili! And for vulnerability management, imagine automated scanning and patching, driven by tools like OpenVAS and Nessus. SRE weaves a proactive net, identifying and mitigating vulnerabilities before attackers can exploit them, transforming weaknesses into mere cracks in the fortress walls, easily sealed before they threaten the core."

He continued; his voice tinged with excitement. "Furthermore, encryption management becomes a seamless part of the system. Imagine automated key rotation and encryption at rest and in transit, powered by tools like Vault and Kubernetes Secrets. SRE ensures data remains an uncrackable cipher, even if attackers breach the outer walls, their spoils rendered useless without the decryption key."

Emili, her eyes gleaming with understanding, pressed on. "So, encryption becomes the hidden vault within the fortress, inaccessible even to the most cunning thieves, their efforts rendered futile against the impenetrable walls of cryptography?"

Soham nodded enthusiastically. "Indeed, Emili! And when incidents inevitably occur, incident response transforms into a well-oiled machine. Imagine automated playbooks, triggered by tools like PagerDuty and VictorOps, mobilizing teams and containing threats with swiftness and precision. SRE ensures every breach is met with a coordinated counteroffensive, minimizing damage and restoring normalcy before attackers can gain a foothold."

A beat of silence hung in the air as he weighed his words. "Finally, even security operation management (SOC) benefits from the SRE lens. Imagine continuous monitoring, automated analysis, and proactive threat hunting, powered by tools like SIEM and XDR. SRE transforms the SOC into a vigilant watchtower, not just reacting to threats, but anticipating them and proactively strengthening defenses against ever-evolving adversaries."

As their conversation reached a crescendo, the hall seemed to thrum with the possibilities unleashed by SRE's transformative impact on various cybersecurity aspects. While threats remain, the application of SRE principles to IAM, vulnerability management, encryption, incident response, and SOC operations offers a compelling vision for a digital fortress where security is not just bolted on but woven into the very fabric of its being.

"Emili," Soham concluded, his voice resonating with conviction, "SRE is not just about tools and practices; it is a philosophy, a way of approaching cybersecurity with proactive resilience. It demands a commitment to automation, vigilance, collaboration, and continuous improvement. Yet, the rewards are undeniable: a fortified digital landscape, minimized risk from cyber threats, and a level of security that inspires confidence and fosters trust in the digital realm."

Soham, his voice still resonating with conviction, continued, "The fortification of our digital realms goes beyond individual practices, Emili. On the horizon, a powerful new wave of resilience washes ashore; the Digital Operational Resilience Act (DORA)." The room held its breath as he paused, his features reflecting the weight of unspoken thoughts. "Europe prepares for a stronger financial shield as DORA mandates a holistic approach to cyber resilience within its institutions. Imagine a framework woven from best practices in incident response, risk management, and third-party vendor oversight, all infused with the automation and vigilance principles of SRE."

He elaborated further, his voice painting a vivid picture. "To bolster their security posture, financial institutions will adopt continuous monitoring technologies, maintain comprehensive incident response protocols, and cultivate a culture of continuous improvement, informed by mandatory vulnerability testing and thorough post-breach investigations. SRE's core principles become embedded within this regulatory framework, transforming financial systems into bastions of resilience, able to withstand even the most sophisticated cyberattacks."

Soham's gaze met Emili's, a knowing smile playing on his lips. "DORA marks a major step forward, Emili. It is not just about compliance; it is about a shared commitment to building a digital ecosystem where resilience is not an aspiration, but an expectation. And within this ecosystem, SRE stands as a potent weapon, its principles guiding the construction of digital fortresses capable of safeguarding not just data and transactions, but also trust and confidence in the very fabric of our digital world."

The hall, once again, seemed to hum with the possibilities unleashed by this potent constructive interaction. DORA, with its regulatory muscle, and SRE, with its agile principles, presented a formidable alliance in the face of ever-evolving cyber threats. The path ahead, illuminated by their combined force, promised a future where digital resilience was not just a theoretical ideal, but a tangible reality, ensuring the impregnability of our digital fortresses for generations to come.

The conversation, having reached a point of profound reflection, naturally paused. The air crackled with unspoken questions, each a potential avenue for further exploration. Emili might delve deeper into the specific provisions of DORA and its implications for SRE implementation, or the focus would shift towards dissecting real-world examples of organizations leveraging DORA and SRE principles to build truly resilient digital infrastructure.

The air, still charged with the possibilities unearthed by DORA and SRE's potent constructive interaction, awaited Emili's next move. Her inquisitive gaze met Soham's, a flicker of curiosity replacing the earlier contemplation.

"Soham," she began, her voice laced with thoughtful inquiry, "DORA's focus on financial institutions is commendable, but its implications surely extend beyond this specific sector. Tell me, how might the principles and regulations have enshrined within DORA ripple outwards, impacting other industries, healthcare, energy, or even critical infrastructure?"

Soham, a knowing smile gracing his lips, gestured towards the imaginary fortress, its walls now adorned with symbols representing various industries. "Ah, Emili, your foresight transcends the surface, illuminating the vast interconnectedness of all things. Indeed, DORA, while initially targeted towards finance, serves as a beacon for other industries, a guiding light illuminating the path towards comprehensive cyber resilience."

He continued, his voice taking on an animated tone. "With DORA's incident response frameworks as their shield, healthcare institutions could orchestrate a symphony of defense against cyberattacks. Imagine patient data and vital equipment shielded from harm, fostering an environment where trust extends beyond financial transactions, encompassing the sacred responsibility of protecting lives."

Emili, her brow furrowed in thoughtful consideration, interjected. "So, DORA's principles become the blueprint for resilience across sectors, ensuring not just financial security, but also safeguarding vital services and protecting human well-being?"

Soham chuckled. "Precisely, Emili! And consider the realm of energy, its infrastructure is a tempting target for malicious actors. Imagine power grids and distribution networks fortified with DORA-inspired resilience measures, equipped with robust anomaly detection, automated remediation strategies, and seamless vendor oversight. Energy systems could transform from vulnerable targets to impregnable fortresses, ensuring uninterrupted power flows, vital for modern societies."

He paused, a thoughtful shadow flickered across his face, momentarily cloaking his expression. "Furthermore, even critical infrastructure, the lifeblood of nations, stands to benefit. Imagine transportation networks, communication systems, and water treatment facilities adopting DORA's proactive approach to risk management. By implementing rigorous vulnerability assessments, continuous monitoring, and stringent third-party vendor vetting, critical infrastructure could become virtually impenetrable, safeguarding the very foundations of our societies."

As their conversation reached a crescendo, the hall seemed to pulse with the possibilities unleashed by DORA's broader implications. While its initial focus lies on finance, its principles and regulations offer a universal roadmap for resilience, empowering diverse industries to construct robust digital fortresses, safeguarding not just financial assets, but also vital services, critical infrastructure, and ultimately, holistic prosperity for all."

"Emili," Soham concluded, his voice resonating with conviction, "DORA is not just a regulation; it is a catalyst for a paradigm shift. It signifies a united effort to forge a digital realm where resilience is not just tackled on but ingrained from the ground up. And by embracing its principles, every industry, every organization, can contribute to weaving a tapestry of interconnected fortresses, a digital ecosystem where security is not just a promise, but a tangible reality."

The conversation, brimming with the transformative potential of DORA's broader impact, reached a natural pause. "Soham," Emili's voice resonated through the dimly lit hall, her gaze unwavering, "Your depiction of DORA's reach across industries paints a compelling picture. Yet, the path to resilience is rarely smooth. Tell me, what specific challenges might differently sectors, like healthcare, energy, and critical infrastructure, face in adopting DORA's principles, and what unique opportunities for enhanced security could each unlock?"

Soham, a knowing smile playing on his lips, gestured towards the imaginary fortress, its walls now segmented, representing distinct industries. "You crack the code and unlock the meaning within, Emili! Each sector, while united in the pursuit of resilience, navigates unique terrains on this journey. Let us explore their landscapes." Diving right in, he highlighted the challenges of healthcare. Outdated systems, complex data privacy rules, and the crucial need for real-time operations call for rapid response with robust data protection in DORA's incident response framework. "It is a tightrope walk, but a necessary one." The room held its breath as he paused, his features reflecting the weight of unspoken thoughts.

Emili furrowed her brow and then cut in, her voice reflecting genuine concern. "The challenge healthcare faces," she began, "is how to be both fast and secure. How can we react to cyberattacks while keeping patient data safe?

Soham chuckled. "Precisely, Emili! Yet, the rewards are undeniable. Imagine healthcare systems adopting continuous monitoring and vulnerability assessments, proactively identifying and mitigating threats before they impact patient care. DORA's principles could transform healthcare IT into a bastion of security and trust, safeguarding not just financial transactions, but human lives."

He shifted his gaze, his voice taking on a new cadence. "Energy, on the other hand, confronts the challenge of geographically dispersed infrastructure, often reliant on aging control systems. Integrating DORA's vendor oversight into complex supply chains and retrofitting legacy systems for automated vulnerability management requires both technical ingenuity and organizational agility."

Emili, her eyes gleaming with understanding, pressed on. "So, energy faces the challenge of integrating resilience measures into geographically diverse and aging infrastructure, requiring both technical expertise and organizational adaptation?"

Soham nodded enthusiastically. "Indeed, Emili! Yet, the potential is immense. Imagine power grids fortified with DORA-inspired anomaly detection, automatically isolating compromised systems, and preventing widespread outages.

Energy systems could become self-healing fortresses, ensuring uninterrupted power flows, vital for modern societies."

He paused, his voice dipped, "the arteries of modern society, from transportation networks to communication grids and water treatment plants, face a complex conundrum. Tightening security without strangling operational effectiveness demands a delicate touch, ensuring these systems remain robust while delivering essential services seamlessly."

Emili, her voice laced with intrigue, leaned forward. "So, critical infrastructure faces the challenge of finding the right balance between security and operational efficiency, ensuring resilience without impacting the very services it is meant to protect?"

Soham chuckled. "Precisely, Emili! Yet, the possibilities are transformative. Imagine transportation networks adopting DORA's risk management principles, proactively identifying and mitigating threats to air travel systems or railway networks. Critical infrastructure could become unbreachable fortresses, safeguarding the very foundations of our societies."

As their conversation reached a crescendo, the hall seemed to thrum with the possibilities unleashed by DORA's challenges and opportunities across diverse industries. While the path to resilience is not without its hurdles, the universal principles enshrined within DORA offer a roadmap for each sector to tailor its digital defenses, transforming itself into a bastion of security, safeguarding not just financial assets, but also vital services, critical infrastructure, and the well-being of individuals and societies.

"Emili," Soham concluded, his voice resonating with conviction, "DORA's journey is not a solitary sprint, but a collaborative marathon. By sharing challenges, fostering knowledge exchange, and adapting DORA's principles to their specific landscapes, every industry can contribute to weaving a tapestry of interconnected resilience, a digital ecosystem where security isn't just a promise, but a shared reality."

"Soham," Emili's voice echoed through the dimly lit hall, her brow furrowed in thoughtful inquiry, "DORA paints a compelling picture of cyber resilience, yet it exists within a landscape already adorned with established industry standards like NIST, ISO, GDPR, and SOX. Tell me, how does DORA weave its threads into this existing tapestry? How does it relate to, complement, or even differ from these familiar frameworks?"

Soham, a hint of knowingness in his eyes, gestured towards the envisioned fortress, its facade now emblazoned with symbols representing various industry standards. "Ah, Emili, your question cuts through the immediate and reveals the intricate interplay between DORA and its fellow guardians of the digital realm! Each framework, while distinct in its focus, contributes to a chorus of security, where DORA acts as the maestro, harmonizing their efforts."

He continued. "The NIST Cybersecurity Framework, for instance, provides a comprehensive roadmap for risk management and cybersecurity best practices. Imagine it as the architectural blueprint for the fortress, laying the cornerstone principles upon which DORA builds its resilient walls. DORA leverages NIST's guidance on incident response, vulnerability management, and supply chain security, amplifying its effectiveness through mandatory implementation and specific regulatory oversight."

Emili, her eyes bright with understanding, interjected. "So, NIST lays the groundwork, and DORA enforces it?"

Soham chuckled. "Precisely! And consider ISO 27001, the global benchmark for information security management systems. Imagine it as the internal security patrol, constantly vigilant and mitigating risks within the fortress walls. DORA strengthens ISO 27001 by mandating specific controls for incident response, vulnerability management, and third-party vendor oversight, bolstering the internal defenses and ensuring continuous vigilance against evolving threats."

He shifted his gaze, his voice taking on a new rhythm. "Take the example of GDPR, the European Union's General Data Protection Regulation. It champions data privacy and user control. Imagine it as the watchful sentinel meticulously vetting any entry and exit of sensitive information from the fortress. DORA aligns with GDPR by emphasizing robust data security measures and incident reporting requirements, ensuring that even in the face of cyberattacks, data privacy remains sacrosanct."

Emili, her brow furrowed in thoughtful contemplation, pressed on. "So, DORA works hand-in-hand with GDPR, ensuring not just operational resilience, but also data privacy, acting as a double layer of protection for sensitive information?"

Soham nodded enthusiastically. "Indeed, Emili! And finally, SOX, the Sarbanes-Oxley Act, focuses on financial reporting accuracy and internal controls. Imagine it as the meticulous auditor, examining every transaction and ensuring financial integrity within the fortress. DORA strengthens SOX by mandating robust incident response and vulnerability management protocols, safeguarding financial systems from cyberattacks that could impact financial reporting and erode trust."

He paused, a thoughtful expression crossing his face. "Let me illustrate this with a tangible example. Imagine a hospital adopting DORA's principles. NIST provides the foundational framework, ISO 27001 ensures continuous internal monitoring, GDPR safeguards patient data privacy, and SOX protects financial integrity. DORA acts as the conductor, harmonizing these efforts and mandating specific actions like incident response drills and vendor oversight, thereby weaving a comprehensive tapestry of cyber resilience and data privacy, protecting not just financial assets but also the lives entrusted to their care."

As their conversation reached its peak, the hall seemed to vibrate with the possibilities unlocked by DORA's synergistic relationship with other industry standards. While each framework plays a distinct role, DORA acts as the catalyst, driving mandatory implementation, synchronizing existing best practices, and ensuring an integrated approach to cyber resilience across diverse sectors.

"Emili," Soham concluded, his voice echoing with conviction, "DORA is not a replacement, but rather a conductor, orchestrating a symphony of security frameworks. It recognizes the value of established best practices while adding the crucial elements of regulatory muscle and mandatory implementation. Together, they form an impregnable fortress against cyber threats, safeguarding not just data and transactions, but also trust and confidence in the very fabric of our digital world."

VIII

Building the Resilient Fortress: Bricks of Policy, Mortar of Framework, and the Spirit of Practice

Emili's piercing gaze met Soham's across the dimly lit hall. The air thrummed with anticipation as she leaned forward, her voice sharpened by the keenness of a seasoned explorer. "Soham," she began, "Your discourse on resilience has woven a compelling tapestry of policies, frameworks, and practices. Yet, within this complex ecosystem, balancing acts and collaborations surely create a fascinating dance of security. Tell me, how do these elements interact? Are there hidden costs woven into robust directives? Can frameworks, however well-intentioned, sometimes create challenges with existing practices? And where, amidst this intertwined interplay, do the sweet spots of constructive collaboration lie, amplifying the overall effectiveness of our cyber defenses?"

Soham, a knowing smile playing on his lips, gestured towards the imaginary fortress, its walls now adorned with symbols representing policies, frameworks, and practices. "Ah, Emili," he chuckled, "Your question delves into the very pulse of cyber resilience! Indeed, these elements exist in an interconnected interplay, where balancing acts and collaborations create a fascinating dance of security."

He continued, his voice taking on an animated tone. "Consider policies, for instance. Imagine them as broad directives, setting overarching goals and mandates for cyber defense. While their intent is undeniable, they can sometimes constrain flexibility. A universal policy might prove ill-suited for diverse organizational needs, potentially hindering the implementation of bespoke solutions in specific contexts."

Emili, her brow furrowed in thoughtful contemplation, interjected. "So, policies, while aiming for comprehensive security, can inadvertently stifle adaptability and creativity in individual systems?"

Soham nodded sagely. "Precisely, Emili! And frameworks, though valuable roadmaps, can also introduce challenges. Imagine them as rigorous guidelines, laying out specific steps and methodologies. While they offer valuable guidance, strict adherence can sometimes stifle creativity and discourage the adoption of emerging practices that might better address evolving threats."

He shifted, a contemplative expression gracing his face. "Yet, amidst these trade-offs, synergies blossom. Policies, when crafted with subtlety and responsiveness, can provide the necessary guardrails while empowering adaptable practices. Frameworks, when used as guiding principles rather than rigid scripts, can spur the creation of context-specific solutions, amplifying the effectiveness of existing practices."

Emili, her eyes alight with understanding, pressed on. "So, the optimal balance lies in policies that empower rather than restrict, and frameworks that inspire adaptation rather than dictate implementation?"

Soham chuckled. "Indeed, Emili! And within this sweet spot, synergies flourish. Imagine policies cultivating an environment of continuous learning and improvement, encouraging the development of innovative practices that address emerging threats. Imagine frameworks serving as launchpads for experimentation, enabling the integration of best practices into existing systems, further strengthening the overall cyber defenses."

He continued, his voice resonating with conviction. "Ultimately, Emili, navigating the interplay of policies, frameworks, and practices is an ongoing journey. By acknowledging the trade-offs, seeking the synergies, and fostering a culture of adaptability and collaboration, we can transform our digital fortresses from rigid structures into dynamic entities, constantly learning and iterating to the ever-changing landscape of cyber threats. In this symphony of resilience, every element, from overarching directives to individual practice, has its role to play. And it is through the harmonious interplay of these elements that we can truly achieve fortified digital defenses."

The hall buzzed with unspoken anticipation of Emili's next question. Her gaze, keen and analytical, met Soham's across the dimly lit space. "Soham," she began, her voice laced with the intrigue of an inquisitive investigator, "Your discourse on cybersecurity's intricate tapestry has unveiled the prominent threads of ISO 27001 and SOC 2. Yet, within this intricate tapestry, synergies and differences surely dance a delicate waltz. Tell me, how do these frameworks blend their voices? Where do their paths diverge, creating unique contributions to the overall security symphony? And, for which orchestras – organizations and their specific needs – does each framework best suit the leadership's direction?"

Soham, an understanding grin playing on his lips, "Your question delves into the very heart of selecting the right security framework! Indeed, ISO 27001 and SOC 2, while both aiming for robust cyber defenses, offer distinct melodies within the grand security symphony." He continued, his voice taking on an animated tone. "Imagine ISO 27001 as the maestro, setting the foundational score for information security management systems (ISMS). It provides a comprehensive framework, laying out a playbook for spotting vulnerabilities, implementing controls, and ensuring continuous vigilance and refinement. Its applicability is universal, making it suitable for any organization regardless of size or industry."

Emili, her forehead creased in thought, interjected. "So, ISO 27001 focuses on building the company-wide security infrastructure, providing a holistic framework for managing and mitigating risks across the entire organization?"

Soham nodded knowingly. "Precisely, Emili! And SOC 2, on the other hand, acts as a focused specialist, concentrating on specific aspects of data security and privacy for service organizations. It offers two distinct approaches, Type 1 and Type 2, each providing varying levels of assurance regarding customer data management."

He paused, a thoughtful expression crossing his face. "The key distinction lies in their scope. ISO 27001 offers a holistic view of your internal security posture, while SOC 2 focuses intensely on data security and privacy specifically relevant to your service offerings and customer trust."

Emili, lit with understanding, pressed on. "So, SOC 2 acts as a dedicated leader for service organizations, focusing on the specific approaches of data security and privacy, ensuring harmony in how customer data is handled?"

Soham chuckled. "Indeed, Emili! And this difference in scope leads to further distinctions. Implementing ISO 27001 can be a complex and resource-intensive undertaking, requiring a dedicated commitment from the organization. SOC 2, on the other hand, can be a streamlined and adaptable solution, ideal for service organizations seeking to demonstrate data security and privacy to their customers."

Soham mused, a hint of amusement twinkling in his eyes. "Ultimately, Emili, the selection between these approaches depends on the specific needs and goals of your organization. If you seek a comprehensive approach to overall information security management, ISO 27001 might be the conductor you need. But if your focus lies on data security and privacy within the context of service offerings, SOC 2's specialized melodies might be the perfect fit. Regardless of your choice, remember that both frameworks contribute valuable notes to the symphony of cyber resilience. By understanding their subtle interaction, you can choose the leader who will harmonize your security measures and lead your organization towards a truly fortified and adaptable digital future."

As their conversation reached its peak, the hall seemed to pulse with the possibilities unleashed by understanding the delicate interaction between ISO 27001 and SOC 2. Emili's insightful inquiries and Soham's comprehensive response offered a valuable guide for navigating this complex terrain, equipping them and anyone listening with the knowledge and perspective to choose the right security framework for their specific needs and orchestrate a robust and resilient digital shield. Emili's gaze, keen and penetrating, cut through the dimly lit hall, finding its mark on Soham across the expanse. A hint of challenge danced in her eyes as she posed her next question. "Soham," her voice resonated, laced with the curiosity of an investigator unraveling a complex map, "Your discourse on cybersecurity's intricate tapestry has revealed the interwoven threads of ISO 27002 and NIST 800-53. Yet, within this complex terrain, synergies and differences surely hold the key to navigating effectively. Tell me, how do these frameworks collaborate effectively? Where do their paths diverge, creating unique contributions to the overall security symphony? And for which orchestras – organizations with their unique needs – does each framework best suit the conductor's baton?"

Soham fell into a contemplative hush, eyes distant as if he were lost in thought. He chuckled, "Your question delves into the very heart of selecting the most suitable security controls! Indeed, ISO 27002 and NIST 800-53, while both aiming to fortify your digital defenses, offer distinct approaches within the grand security symphony."

He continued, his voice taking on an animated tone. "Imagine ISO 27002 as the seasoned director, wielding a comprehensive library of the most widely recognized information security controls. It provides an overarching blueprint, outlining a proven set of safeguards to address various security risks. Its focus lies on established methodologies, applicable to any organization regardless of size or industry."

Emili, her brow wrinkled in thought, interjected. "So, ISO 27002 acts as the experienced director, offering a well-established playbook of security controls, ensuring organizations can select the most suitable safeguards for their specific needs?"

Soham nodded sagely. "Precisely, Emili! And NIST 800-53, on the other hand, acts as a sector-specific architect, offering an extensive repository of security controls tailored to specific sectors and government requirements. It delves deeper into the implementation details, providing detailed instructions on crafting and customizing controls to address unique threats and vulnerabilities."

He paused, a thoughtful expression crossing his face. "The key difference lies in their level of specificity. ISO 27002 offers an adaptable framework, while NIST 800-53 provides a rigorous blueprint."

Emili, her eyes gleaming with understanding, pressed on. "So, NIST 800-53 acts as the specialist composer, crafting customized security melodies for specific sectors and needs, ensuring a more targeted and nuanced approach to addressing threats?"

Soham amused himself with a chuckle. "Indeed, Emili! And these differing approaches lead to further differentiations. Choosing ISO 27002 can be straightforward, offering an easily accessible set of best practices. However, navigating NIST 800-53 requires careful consideration due to its extensive scope and sector-specific focus. Selecting the relevant controls and customizing them to your unique context can be a complex undertaking."

He concluded firmly, his voice resonating with conviction. "Ultimately, Emili, the choice between these frameworks hinges on the specific needs and priorities of your organization. If you seek an easily accessible set of best practices for building a fortified security foundation, ISO 27002 could be the ideal leader for you. But if your requirements demand a more detailed and sector-specific approach, NIST 800-53's tailored solutions might be the perfect fit. Regardless of your choice, remember that both frameworks contribute valuable notes to the symphony of cyber resilience. By understanding their subtle interaction, you can choose the leader who will harmonize your security controls and lead your organization towards a truly fortified and adaptable digital shield."

The tranquil silence evaporated in an instant, replaced by Emili's words. "Soham," her voice laced with the keenness of a seasoned explorer, "Your discourse on weaving policies into the fabric of resilience has been captivating. Yet, policies often remain abstract entities, pronouncements echoing in lofty halls. Tell me, how do these pronouncements translate into concrete action?

Soham, a knowing smile gracing his appearance, responded, "Your question delves into the very heart of policy implementation! Indeed, translating broad goals into actionable clauses is where the rubber meets the road in the quest for resilient systems."

He shifted in his seat, his voice taking on an animated tone. "Imagine, for instance, a policy clause mandating continuous vulnerability assessments. This would not simply be a lofty statement about the importance of identifying security flaws. It would translate into concrete actions – regular scans of systems, defined procedures for prioritizing and remediating vulnerabilities, and clear escalation protocols for critical issues."

Emili, her brow furrowed in thoughtful contemplation, interjected. "So, this clause becomes the orchestra conductor, directing the team in a coordinated dance of identification, prioritization, and remediation, ensuring vulnerabilities don't linger in the shadows."

Soham chuckled. "Precisely, Emili! And consider another clause – one mandating incident response preparedness. This would not just be a call for vigilance. It would necessitate the creation of detailed incident response plans, outlining roles and responsibilities, communication protocols, and recovery procedures specific to different types of cyberattacks."

He paused, a thoughtful expression crossing his face. "Imagine this clause as the emergency fire alarm, jolting the organization into action with clear instructions and defined steps to contain the damage, minimize disruption, and swiftly restore normalcy."

Emili, her eyes gleaming with understanding, pressed on. "So, this clause acts as the emergency protocol, ensuring everyone knows their role and the right actions to take, transforming chaos into a coordinated response in the face of cyber threats."

Soham nodded enthusiastically. "Indeed, Emili! And beyond technical safeguards, policies can also foster a culture of resilience. Imagine a clause mandating employee security awareness training. This would not just be a checkbox exercise. It would involve regular training sessions, simulated phishing attacks, and ongoing communication campaigns, ensuring everyone within the organization understands their role in cyber defense."

Soham responded, his voice resonating with conviction. "These are just a few examples, Emili, but they illustrate the power of translating broad goals into concrete policy clauses. By weaving these clauses into the very fabric of an organization, we transform resilience from an abstract ideal into a living, breathing reality. Each clause becomes a thread in the tapestry of defense, a note in the symphony of security, ensuring our digital fortresses stand tall against the ever-evolving landscape of cyber threats."

"Soham," her voice laced with the urgency of a seasoned explorer navigating uncharted territory, "your explanation of the complex web of cyber resilience has shed light on the crucial role of data security. But within this intricate landscape, frameworks like NIST, ISO, GDPR, and DORA speak different languages. Can you explain how these frameworks collaborate when it comes to data security? Where do their approaches differ, creating unique contributions to the overall security strategy? And most importantly, which framework is best suited to conduct the data security orchestra for different organizations, given their individual security postures?"

Soham, a hint of playful wisdom in his eyes, gestured towards the imaginary fortress now bearing the insignia of data security heavyweights: NIST, ISO, ISO 27001, GDPR, and DORA. "Ah, Emili," he chuckled, "your question pierces the very core of safeguarding the digital age's most prized possession - data! While these frameworks all strive for data security, they orchestrate distinct melodies within the grand symphony of data protection."

His voice adopted a lively cadence. "Think of NIST Cybersecurity Framework and ISO 27001 as the foundational maestros, crafting the overarching score for information security management systems (ISMS). They serve as comprehensive frameworks, outlining best practices for data security controls, risk management, and incident response. Their focus is broad, encompassing organizations of all sizes and industries."

Emili, her brow furrowed in thoughtful contemplation, interjected. "So, NIST and ISO act as the experienced maestros, offering a well-rehearsed repertoire of data security controls, ensuring organizations can select the most effective measures for their specific data protection needs?"

Soham nodded sagely. "Precisely, Emili! And GDPR, on the other hand, acts as a specialized composer, crafting a powerful melody focused on individual data privacy rights. It mandates transparency, control, and accountability for organizations handling personal data within the European Union. Its focus is granular, empowering individuals with control over their data and imposing strict regulations on its collection, storage, and processing."

He paused, a thoughtful expression crossing his face. "The key difference lies in their scope and emphasis. NIST and ISO offer a broad foundation for data security controls, while GDPR delves deep into individual privacy rights and regulatory compliance."

Emili, her eyes gleaming with understanding, pressed on. "So, GDPR acts as the champion of individual autonomy, ensuring organizations harmonize their data security measures with the right notes of transparency, control, and accountability for data subjects?"

Soham chuckled. "Indeed, Emili! And DORA, the newest conductor on the stage, brings a distinct melody focused on operational resilience in the financial sector. It mandates robust data security measures for financial institutions, emphasizing incident reporting, vulnerability management, and third-party vendor oversight. Its focus is on ensuring financial systems and data remain resilient in the face of cyberattacks."

"Ultimately, Emili, the choice of framework, or rather the combination of frameworks, depends on the specific data security needs and regulatory landscape of your organization. If you seek a broad foundation for data security controls, NIST and ISO might be the maestros you need. But if your data falls under GDPR's purview, harmonizing your data security measures with its privacy-centric melody is paramount. And for financial institutions, DORA's emphasis on operational resilience becomes the essential conductor's baton. Remember, each framework contributes valuable notes to the symphony of data security. By understanding their synergies and differences, you can choose the right conductors and orchestrate a truly robust and resilient data protection posture for your organization."

Emili's sharp gaze pierced through the hall's dimness, locking onto Soham across the distance. A spark of curiosity ignited in her eyes as she embarked on her next inquiry. "Soham," her voice resonated, imbued with the inquisitive spirit of a trailblazer entering unknown lands, "Your exploration of cyber resilience has illuminated the intricate fabric woven by software security. But within this complex terrain, frameworks like NIST, ISO, GDPR, and DORA establish their own unique narratives, dictating diverse approaches. Tell me, how do these narratives synchronize their themes when it comes to safeguarding our software? Where do their paths diverge, composing distinct verses within the overarching poem of security? For which software architects – development teams with their individual needs – does each framework best serve as the guiding editor?"

Soham, a knowing smile playing on his lips, gestured towards the imaginary fortress, its walls now adorned with parchments representing clauses from NIST, ISO, SECURE, GDPR, and DORA. "Ah, Emili," he chuckled, "Your question delves into the very core of building secure software, the foundation upon which our digital world rests! Indeed, these frameworks, while all aiming for robust software security, offer distinct verses within the grand security epic."

He continued, his voice taking on an animated tone. "Imagine NIST Cybersecurity Framework and ISO 27001 as the seasoned editors, providing foundational guidance through clauses on secure coding practices, vulnerability management, and supply chain security. They offer a comprehensive script, applicable to any software development team regardless of the software's purpose or complexity."

Emili, her brow furrowed in thoughtful contemplation, interjected. "So, NIST and ISO act as the experienced guides, offering well-rehearsed stanzas on secure development methodologies, ensuring software development teams have the tools and processes to build secure software from the ground up?"

Soham nodded sagely. "Precisely! The key difference lies in their depth and emphasis. NIST and ISO offer a broad foundation for secure software development practices, while SECURE dives deep into specific SDLC stages, ensuring meticulous security considerations at every step. And GDPR, on the other hand, champions individual privacy, adds a distinct verse focused on data protection.

Its clauses mandate privacy-by-design principles, data minimization practices, and robust data security controls, ensuring software handles personal data with utmost respect and accountability."

Soham's voice resonated with conviction. "Finally, DORA, the newest conductor on the stage, brings a powerful stanza focused on operational resilience in software used by financial institutions. Its clauses mandate secure coding practices for financial software, vulnerability management in third-party dependencies, and incident reporting for software-related threats, ensuring financial systems and data remain resilient in the face of cyberattacks."

"Ultimately, Emili, the choice of framework, or rather the combination of frameworks, depends on the specific software security needs and regulatory landscape of your development team. If you seek a broad foundation for secure development practices, NIST and ISO might be the editors you need. But if your software handles sensitive data, harmonizing your development process with GDPR's privacy-centric verses is paramount. And for financial software, DORA's emphasis on operational resilience becomes the essential editor's pen. Remember, each framework contributes valuable stanzas to the epic of secure software. By understanding their synergies and differences, your development team can choose the right editors and craft a truly secure and resilient software masterpiece."

Emili's gaze, ever sharp, met Soham's across the dimly lit hall. A hint of challenge flickered in her eyes as she posed her next question. "Soham," her voice resonated, laced with the inquisitive spirit of an explorer peering beyond the horizon, "Your discourse on the intricate tapestry of cyber resilience has painted a vivid picture of internal defenses and software fortresses. Yet, one thread seems curiously absent – the very fabric upon which these structures rely. Tell me, is it truly enough to fortify our own walls? Should we not cast our gaze outward, towards the supply chains that nourish our digital ecosystems? Is supply chain security merely a footnote in the grand epic of resilience, or does it warrant a full-fledged chapter of its own?"

Soham, a knowing smile playing on his lips, gestured towards the imaginary fortress, its walls now adorned with a question mark hovering above the intricate supply chain network feeding into it. "Ah, Emili," he chuckled, "Your question delves into the very heart of a vulnerability often overlooked – the Achilles' heel of even the most robust defenses. Indeed, supply chain security is not a mere footnote, but rather the prologue to the epic of resilience. For even the strongest walls crumble if the stones upon which they are built are riddled with flaws."

He continued, his voice taking on an animated tone. "Imagine your digital infrastructure as a magnificent castle, its towers reaching for the sky. Yet, if the quarries providing the stone for its construction are infiltrated, if the tools used by the masons are compromised, if even the carts transporting the materials are tampered with, the entire edifice remains vulnerable. Supply chain security is the watchful guard at the quarry, the vigilant inspector of tools, the protector of every step in the journey from raw materials to final construction, ensuring the entire ecosystem is free from malicious intent and hidden vulnerabilities."

Emili, her brow furrowed in thoughtful contemplation, interjected. "So, supply chain security acts as the vigilant sentinel, safeguarding the very foundation of our digital ecosystems, ensuring that every component, from the smallest screw to the grandest software package, arrives untainted and trustworthy?"

Soham nodded sagely. "Precisely. And the consequences of neglecting this sentinel are dire. Compromised software dependencies can introduce backdoors into your systems, tainted hardware can harbor hidden exploits, and malicious actors within the supply chain can manipulate data or disrupt operations. Supply chain security is not an option, it is the cornerstone of building truly resilient digital fortresses."

As their conversation reached a crescendo, the hall was illuminated by their shared pursuit of a secure and resilient digital future.

IX

Building Bridges, Not Backdoors: Fostering Collaboration and Trust in the Digital Ecosystem

The room buzzed with hushed anticipation as Emili's keen gaze, undimmed by the dimly lit space, locked onto Soham across the table. Emili's voice, brimming with the curiosity of a trailblazer venturing into unknown lands, pierced the silence. "Soham," she began, "your exploration of cyber resilience has beautifully painted a picture of robust fortresses and watchful guardians. But one thread seems curiously under-examined – the very lifeblood of these digital ecosystems, their supply chains. Tell me, what mysteries lie hidden within this realm of 'Supply Chain Security'? And why, in your expert opinion, does it deserve such a prominent role in the grand narrative of resilience?"

Smiling knowingly, he gestures towards the imaginary fortress. Now, a question mark hangs in the air, hovering above the complex network of suppliers and dependencies feeding into it. "Emili," he chuckles, "your question strikes at the core of a frequently underestimated vulnerability – the unseen weak spot hidden even within the strongest defenses. As you rightly pointed out, supply chain security is not just an afterthought, it is the very foundation of building true resilience. Allow me to illuminate its critical importance

He leaned forward, his voice taking on an animated tone. "Imagine your digital infrastructure as a magnificent castle, its towers reaching for the sky. Yet, if the quarries providing the stone for its construction are infiltrated, if the tools used by the masons are compromised, if even the carts transporting the materials are tampered with, the entire edifice remains vulnerable. Supply Chain Security acts as the watchful guard at the quarry, the vigilant inspector of tools, the protector of every step in the journey from raw materials to final construction, ensuring the entire ecosystem is free from malicious intent and hidden vulnerabilities."

Emili, her brow furrowed in thoughtful contemplation, interjected. "So, Supply Chain Security acts as the vigilant sentinel, safeguarding the very foundation of our digital ecosystems, ensuring that every component, from the smallest screw to the grandest software package, arrives untainted and trustworthy?"

Soham nodded sagely. "Precisely! And the consequences of neglecting this sentinel are dire. Compromised software dependencies can introduce backdoors into your systems, tainted hardware can harbor hidden exploits, and malicious actors within the supply chain can manipulate data or disrupt operations. Supply Chain Security is not an option, it is the cornerstone of building truly resilient digital fortresses."

As their conversation reached a crescendo, the hall seemed to hum with the newfound understanding of the critical role Supply Chain Security plays in building digital resilience. Emili's insightful question and Soham's comprehensive response offered a compelling argument for elevating Supply Chain Security beyond a footnote, paving the way for a deeper exploration of this crucial aspect of cyber defense and its potential to safeguard the foundations of our digital world.

Emili curiously said, "So, supply chain security means vetting vendors, securing software dependencies, and monitoring the entire ecosystem for threats." Is not it?"

"Yes, for only by weaving Supply Chain Security into the very fabric of our digital defenses can we hope to stand tall in the face of ever-evolving cyber threats and build a truly resilient future for all."

The embers of curiosity flickered brightly in Emili's eyes as she met Soham's gaze across the dimly lit hall. "Your words, Soham," she began, her voice laced with the urgency of an explorer nearing a hidden valley, "have painted a vivid picture of the vital role Supply Chain Security plays in our digital resilience. Yet, within this valley lie myriad paths, each leading to distinct aspects of this crucial domain. Tell me, where do we begin? What are the essential threads we must weave into this tapestry of secure supply chains?"

Soham, a knowing smile playing on his lips, gestured towards the imaginary fortress, its walls now adorned with intricate pathways representing various aspects of Supply Chain Security. "Your thirst for knowledge is akin to navigating a complex map, seeking to chart the course towards true digital resilience. And indeed, Supply Chain Security offers a multitude of paths, each vital in safeguarding the foundations of our digital ecosystems", he concluded.

He paused, his gaze sweeping across the pathways. "Firstly, let us explore the bedrock of any robust security posture – best practices and policies. Imagine these as the sturdy stones upon which our defenses are built. We must implement vendor vetting procedures, meticulously assessing our suppliers' security practices and track records. Software dependency management becomes paramount, ensuring the integrity and security of every code snippet woven into our systems. And let us not forget the importance of secure coding practices throughout the entire supply chain, from conception to deployment."

Emili, her brow furrowed in thought, interjected. "So, these policies and practices act as the blueprints and guidelines, dictating how we vet our partners, manage dependencies, and ensure secure coding across the entire supply chain landscape?"

Soham nodded enthusiastically. "Precisely, Emili! And to complement these blueprints, we must equip ourselves with the right tools and technologies – the skilled artisans shaping our secure supply chains. Vulnerability scanning tools become our watchful eyes, identifying weaknesses within software dependencies and hardware components. Continuous monitoring solutions act as vigilant sentinels, constantly scanning the supply chain for suspicious activity and potential threats."

He continued, his voice taking on an animated tone. "Furthermore, blockchain technology emerges as a revolutionary tool, enabling tamper-proof tracking of software provenance and ensuring the authenticity of every component within the supply chain. And let us not underestimate the power of collaboration and information sharing. By fostering open communication and threat intelligence exchange across industries and organizations, we can collectively strengthen the entire digital ecosystem."

Emili, her eyes gleaming with understanding, pressed on. "So, these tools and technologies act as the instruments and techniques in our hands, allowing us to scan for vulnerabilities, monitor for threats, leverage blockchain for authenticity, and collaborate across the industry to build a more resilient digital landscape?"

"Indeed," Soham affirmed, "And remember, this is not an exhaustive list, but rather a compass guiding us through the multifaceted terrain of Supply Chain Security. As we delve deeper into specific aspects, such as securing hardware components, managing open-source dependencies, or mitigating insider threats, we will encounter even more tools, best practices, and technological advancements shaping the future of this critical domain."

The hall hummed with the quiet energy of intellectual pursuit as Emili's gaze, ever discerning, met Soham's across the dimly lit space. A hint of inquiry danced in her eyes as she posed her next question. "Soham," her voice resonated, laced with the curiosity of an explorer navigating uncharted territory, "Your discourse on the intricate tapestry of supply chain security has unveiled the vital threads of best practices and technological advancements. Yet, within this landscape, do formal structures exist? Are there regulatory frameworks, akin to NIST or its brethren, that guide and govern these crucial cybersecurity efforts?"

Soham, a knowing smile playing on his lips, gestured towards the imaginary fortress, its walls now adorned with parchments representing various cybersecurity regulations and frameworks. "Ah, Emili, your question delves into the very framework upon which a secure supply chain rest! Indeed, while best practices and tools form the mortar and bricks, regulations and frameworks act as the guiding blueprints, establishing the standards and expectations for secure supply chain practices."

He continued, his voice taking on an animated tone. "Imagine NIST SP 884, 'Supplier Risk Management Practices for Federal Information Systems and Organizations'. This framework serves as a comprehensive guide for government agencies, outlining best practices for vendor vetting, security assessments, and risk mitigation throughout the supply chain."

Emili, her brow furrowed in thoughtful contemplation, interjected. "So, NIST SP 884 acts as a well-worn map, guiding organizations through the process of assessing and mitigating supplier risks, ensuring secure partnerships and trustworthy components within their supply chains?"

Soham nodded astutely. "Precisely! And beyond NIST, other frameworks like CSA STAR and CISA's Cybersecurity Maturity Model for Supply Chain Management (CMMC) offer complementary perspectives. CSA STAR focuses on security assessments of software vendors, while CMMC emphasizes maturity levels for defense contractors' cybersecurity practices throughout their supply chains."

He paused, a thoughtful expression crossing his face. "The key difference lies in their scope and emphasis. NIST SP 884 offers a broad framework for government agencies, while CSA STAR and CMMC cater to specific industries and requirements."

Emili, her eyes gleaming with understanding, pressed on. "So, these frameworks act as specialized architects, each offering blueprints tailored to different needs? NIST for government agencies, CSA STAR for software vendors, and CMMC for defense contractors, ensuring robust security practices across diverse supply chain landscapes?"

Soham chuckled. "Indeed! And remember, regulations and frameworks are not static entities. They constantly evolve to keep pace with the ever-changing threat landscape. Emerging regulations like the EU's proposed Supply Chain Due Diligence Act and the UK's Security of Supply Chain regulations further emphasize the importance of secure supply chains across industries and borders."

He concluded, his voice resonating with conviction. "Therefore, Emili, staying abreast of these evolving regulations and frameworks is crucial for building truly resilient digital ecosystems. By leveraging their guidance and tailoring them to your specific needs, you can ensure your supply chain is not only secure but also compliant with relevant regulations, paving the way for a more trustworthy and resilient digital future for all." Emili, with her curious gazes, "So, how in general do organizations start their supply chain security journey?"

Soham responded enthusiastically, "Emili, that's a fantastic question, and one that's becoming increasingly important for organizations of all sizes. Starting your supply chain security journey can feel daunting, but by breaking it down into stages and focusing on key areas, you can make quick progress in mitigating risk. Think of this as laying the groundwork. First, it is crucial to understand your organization's software supply chain: who your vendors are, what components they provide, and how they integrate into your systems. This is where tools like Software Bill of Materials (SBOM) come in handy, giving you a clear picture of your attack surface.

"Next, identify key threats like malicious code injection, unauthorized access, or data breaches throughout the supply chain. Knowing your vulnerabilities helps you prioritize security controls. Now it is time to put up some defenses! Start with secure coding practices from your vendors and within your own organization. Encourage the use of well-maintained, reputable libraries and components. Implement vulnerability scanning at regular intervals to identify and patch weaknesses promptly."

Soham took a brief pause. "Don't forget about access controls: restrict access to sensitive systems and data and enforce multi-factor authentication where possible. Consider continuous monitoring solutions to keep an eye on suspicious activity throughout your supply chain. Security is an ongoing journey, Emili, not a destination. Regularly review and update your security policies based on evolving threats and industry best practices. Conduct periodic audits to assess the effectiveness of your controls and identify areas for improvement."

"Remember", Soham said wisely, "communication is the key. Collaborate with your vendors and partners to establish shared security practices and responsibilities. Encourage information sharing about vulnerabilities and incidents to stay ahead of the curve. By following these stages and focusing on awareness, safeguards, and continuous improvement, you can build a robust supply chain security posture that protects your organization and its data. It is not a sprint, but a marathon, and every step you take strengthens your defenses against ever-growing threats".

The room was buzzing with newfound awareness of the vital role regulations and frameworks play in constructing secure supply chains. Emili's astute inquiry and Soham's insightful response had illuminated this cornerstone of cyber resilience, empowering them with the knowledge and perspective to navigate the ever-shifting regulatory landscape.

X

Shifting Tides: A Shared Journey of Growth Begins

The embers of their intellectual fire still glowed in the dimly lit hall as Emili met Soham's gaze across the space. A hint of introspection danced in her eyes as she posed her question, her voice laced with thoughtful curiosity. "Soham," she began, her words echoing with the weight of unspoken possibilities, "Your discourse has painted a magnificent canvas of cybersecurity mastery. Your expertise weaves intricate tapestries of defense, your strategies gleam like polished armor against the ever-evolving digital threats. Yet, within this fortress of knowledge, I find myself pondering your own placement. Tell me, where do you see yourself within this grand narrative of resilience? Are you the architect, meticulously designing the defenses? Or the vigilant sentinel, ever watchful on the ramparts? Or do you envision yourself as something else entirely?"

Soham, a knowing smile playing on his lips, leaned back in his chair, relishing the depth of Emili's inquiry. "Your question delves into the very heart of purpose, the driving force that fuels our endeavors in this digital battlefield. Indeed, the roles you propose are each vital, yet I find myself drawn to a slightly different perspective."

He paused, his gaze sweeping across the imagined fortress, his voice taking on a contemplative tone. "Imagine me not as the architect, dictating blueprints from on high, but rather as the skilled craftsman, hands-on in the trenches, shaping defenses alongside my comrades. I envision myself as the mentor, the guide who shares knowledge and experience, empowering others to forge their own paths of resilience."

Emili, her brow furrowed in thought, interjected. "So, you see yourself as a catalyst, igniting the spark of understanding within others, enabling them to build their own fortresses of cybersecurity awareness?"

Soham nodded enthusiastically. "Precisely, Emili! My greatest satisfaction lies not in wielding expertise like a solitary weapon, but in empowering others to wield their own knowledge with confidence and skill. I aspire to be the bridge between theory and practice, the guiding hand that transforms potential into unwavering resilience."

He continued, his voice resonating with conviction. "Perhaps I am also the storyteller, weaving cautionary tales of breaches and triumphs, ensuring the lessons learned echo across generations of digital defenders. For ultimately, Emili, the true strength of our defenses lies not in any one individual, but in the collective knowledge, vigilance, and unwavering collaboration of those who stand guard against the ever-evolving digital threats."

As their conversation reached a climax, the hall seemed to pulse with the newfound understanding of Soham's self-perceived role. Emili's insightful question and Soham's comprehensive response had offered a glimpse into his motivations and aspirations, revealing a multifaceted vision of mentorship, collaboration, and shared knowledge as the true cornerstone of digital resilience.

The path ahead, illuminated by their shared pursuit of a secure and resilient future, held the promise of further exploration into specific ways Soham envisioned enacting his role, real-world examples displaying the impact of collaborative cybersecurity efforts, and even a dive into the emerging trends and technologies shaping the future of knowledge sharing and collective defense in the digital landscape.

The embers of their intellectual fire still flickered in the dimly lit hall as Emili met Soham's gaze across space. A hint of melancholy danced in her eyes as she spoke, her voice laced with bittersweet admiration. "Soham," she began, the words heavy with unspoken emotions, " The flow of your thoughts was like a captivating melody, each point building upon the last, each verse weaving intricate tapestries of cybersecurity wisdom. Your depth of understanding and breadth of experience are beyond compare, a fortress of expertise against the ever-evolving threats of the digital age."

The air in the dimly lit interview room crackled with a subtle tension. Emili, her gaze sharp as ever, leaned across the table, her voice laced with polite skepticism.

"Soham," she began, "Your discourse has indeed been impressive. Your understanding of the cyber landscape is vast, your insights into threat vectors keen. However, due to this position's critical nature, I must ask about your formal qualifications. Do you possess any industry-recognized cybersecurity certifications?"

Soham, a flicker of discomfort momentarily crossing his face, met her gaze with unwavering confidence. "While I hold no specific certifications, Emili," he conceded, "my expertise stems from a different crucible. Years of hands-on experience in the trenches, battling real-world threats across diverse industries, have honed my skills far beyond the confines of textbook knowledge."

He paused, his voice taking on a measured tone. "Think of certifications as maps, valuable guides to navigate the terrain. Yet, my experience has been my compass, forged in the fires of countless skirmishes, guiding me through uncharted territory, adapting to ever-evolving threats."

Emili, her brow furrowed in contemplation, tapped her pen against the table. "But surely, Soham," she countered, "formal training and validation through recognized certifications offer a certain level of assurance. They provide tangible proof of expertise, a standardized yardstick to measure one's preparedness against established benchmarks."

Soham nodded patiently. "I understand your perspective, Emili. Certifications hold their merit, providing a structured framework for knowledge acquisition. However, they often paint a static picture, failing to capture the dynamism of the real world, the constant evolution of threats and vulnerabilities."

He leaned forward, his eyes glinting with conviction. "True expertise, in my experience, lies not in memorized formulas or standardized tests, but in the scars of battle, the ingenuity forged in the face of the unknown. It lies in the ability to think critically, adapt on the fly, and craft bespoke solutions for ever-shifting challenges."

The cybersecurity landscape isn't a battlefield with predetermined rules of engagement," he continued. "It's an ever-shifting maze, where attackers don't wait for certifications to catch up. My value lies in recognizing patterns others might miss, anticipating moves before they're made, and devising solutions tailored to this threat, to your organization, right now."

Soham leaned a bit closer, a hint of challenge in his smile. "Perhaps you could consider my lack of certifications as an advantage, Emili. My mind is unburdened by the biases that formalized knowledge sometimes creates. I see possibilities others overlook because they're too focused on established checklists."

He sat back, letting the impact of his words settle. "I'm not dismissing the value of a good credential, but when your company's on the line, do you want someone who aced a multiple-choice test, or someone who's proven themselves in the heat of the moment?"

Suddenly, all conversation ceased. The only sound was the distant whirring of the building's systems. Emili, her gaze now tinged with newfound respect, considered Soham's words. The weight of her decision, the potential consequences of prioritizing certifications over raw talent, pressed upon her.

Finally, she met his gaze, a resolute gleam replacing her earlier skepticism. "Soham," she conceded, "Your argument holds merit. In this instance, experience truly is the ultimate teacher. I am willing to take a chance, to see beyond the limitations of standardized tests and trust in the crucible forged in your actual battles."

Soham, a genuine smile gracing his features, extended his hand. "A wise decision, Emili," he replied, a newfound respect echoing in his voice. "Together, perhaps we can rewrite the narrative, where experience and talent find their rightful place alongside formal validation, paving the way for a more nuanced, more effective approach to cybersecurity."

As their hands clasped, the air in the room seemed to lighten, the tension replaced by a shared sense of understanding and cautious optimism. Emili's decision, a bold step against the tide of conventional hiring practices, had opened the door to a future where raw talent, honed through hard-won experience, could stand shoulder-to-shoulder with formal credentials, building a more resilient and dynamic line of defense against the ever-evolving threats of the digital age.

The path ahead, illuminated by their shared commitment to excellence, held the promise of further exploration into alternative forms of talent evaluation, real-world success stories highlighting the impact of experience-driven expertise, and even a shift in the industry's approach to recognizing and nurturing the value of practical knowledge in the face of ever-growing cyber threats.

BEYOND THE SCOREBOARD: REDEFINING TALENT IN THE AGE OF AI

In the dimly lit interview room, Emili's measured appreciation met Soham's battle-forged confidence, igniting a spark of debate that transcended the confines of a single hiring decision. Their discourse, echoing far beyond the walls, laid bare a critical truth – in the face of ever-evolving digital threats, our overreliance on academic accolades risks obscuring the true gems: individuals honed by the furnace of experience.

The sterile landscape of standardized tests and rigid curricula often fails to capture the dynamism of the real world. Soham, the embodiment of this uncharted territory, navigated the labyrinthine complexities of cybersecurity not through textbook theorems, but through the scars of countless skirmishes, the ingenuity forged in the crucible of real-world threats. His expertise, etched in the lines of his weathered face, resonated with a truth Emili, blinded by the allure of certifications, had almost missed.

This, however, is not an isolated incident. We live in a world where the currency of talent is often measured by the gleam of degrees and the clink of perfect scores. We prioritize the veneer of academic achievement over the grit of on-the-ground experience, relegating the wisdom gleaned from practical application to the shadows. This myopic focus not only stifles individual potential but also jeopardizes our collective future, especially in a domain as critical as cybersecurity.

The digital age, intricately woven with the threads of artificial intelligence, demands a change in thinking in how we nurture talent. In this interconnected web, where algorithms hold sway and data reigns supreme, mere bookish knowledge is a blunt instrument against the ever-morphing arsenal of cyber threats. We need individuals who can think outside the rigid boxes of standardized tests, who can adapt and innovate in the face of the unknown, and who possess the critical thinking skills to outmaneuver the cunning machinations of AI-powered adversaries.

Experience-based learning, therefore, must become the cornerstone of our talent development strategies. Mentorship programs, apprenticeships, and hands-on projects must replace the monotonous drone of rote learning. We must empower individuals to learn by doing, to fail and iterate, to navigate the messy complexities of the real world where theoretical frameworks often crumble and solutions demand ingenuity, not formulas.

This is not to diminish the value of academic rigor. Knowledge remains the bedrock upon which practical application thrives. However, it is the fusion of these two worlds, the harmonious marriage of theory and practice, that unlocks the true potential of talent. In the realm of cybersecurity, where a single misstep can have catastrophic consequences, experience becomes the essential seasoning that tempers theoretical knowledge, transforming it into a potent shield against the ever-present digital storms.

Emili's decision to look beyond the sterile confines of certifications and recognize the wisdom etched in Soham's experience serves as a beacon of hope. It demonstrates a willingness to redefine talent, to move beyond the limitations of traditional metrics and embrace the dynamism of lived experience. As we step deeper into the age of AI, where the lines between the virtual and real blur, it is this very willingness to adapt and embrace new paradigms that will determine our resilience, our ability to not only survive but thrive in the face of unprecedented challenges.

The echoes of Soham and Emili's conversation, amplified by the urgent need for cybersecurity expertise in a world ruled by AI, call for a radical shift in our approach to talent development. Let us move beyond the tyranny of the scoreboard, celebrate the wisdom gleaned from experience, and empower individuals to navigate the uncharted territories of the digital age. For in the crucible of experience, not the sterility of standardized tests, lies the true fount of talent, the bedrock upon which we can build a future secure from the shadows of the digital unknown.